PRAISE FOR

Top 10 Romance of 2012, 2015, and 2016.

— BOOKLIST: THE NIGHT IS MINE, HOT POINT,
HEART STRIKE

One of our favorite authors.

— RT BOOK REVIEWS

Buchman has catapulted his way to the top tier of my favorite authors.

— FRESH FICTION

A favorite author of mine. I'll read anything that carries his name, no questions asked. Meet your new favorite author!

— THE SASSY BOOKSTER, FLASH OF FIRE

M.L. Buchman is guaranteed to get me lost in a good story.

— THE READING CAFE, WAY OF THE WARRIOR:
NSDQ

I love Buchman's writing. His vivid descriptions bring everything to life in an unforgettable way.

— PURE JONEL, HOT POINT

OFF THE LEASH

A WHITE HOUSE PROTECTION FORCE ROMANCE

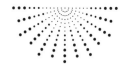

M. L. BUCHMAN

Buchman Bookworks

Other works by M. L. Buchman:

CHAPTER ONE

"Y ou're joking."

"Nope. That's his name. And he's yours now."

Sergeant Linda Hamlin wondered quite what it would take to wipe that smile off Lieutenant Jurgen's face. A 120mm round from an M1A1 Abrams Main Battle Tank came to mind.

The kennel master of the US Secret Service's Canine Team was clearly a misogynistic jerk from the top of his polished head to the bottoms of his equally polished boots. She wondered if the shoelaces were polished as well.

Then she looked over at the poor dog sitting hopefully on the concrete kennel floor. His stall had a dog bed three times his size and a water bowl deep enough for him to bathe in. No toys, because toys always came from the handler as a reward. He offered her a sad sigh and a liquid doggy gaze. The kennel even smelled wrong, more of sanitizer than dog. The walls seemed to echo with each bark down the long line of kennels housing the candidate hopefuls for the next addition to the Secret Service's team.

Thor—really?—was a brindle-colored mutt, part who-knew

1

and part no-one-cared. He looked like a cross between an oversized, long-haired schnauzer and a dust mop that someone had spilled dark gray paint on. After mixing in streaks of tawny brown, they'd left one white paw just to make him all the more laughable.

And of course Lieutenant Jerk Jurgen would assign Thor to the first woman on the USSS K-9 team.

Unable to resist, she leaned over far enough to scruff the dog's ears. He was the physical opposite of the sleek and powerful Malinois MWDs—military war dogs—that she'd been handling for the 75th Rangers for the last five years. They twitched with eagerness and nerves. A good MWD was seventy pounds of pure drive—every damn second of the day. If the mild-mannered Thor weighed thirty pounds, she'd be surprised. And he looked like a little girl's best friend who should have a pink bow on his collar.

Jurgen was clearly ex-Marine and would have no respect for the Army. Of course, having been in the Army's Special Operations Forces, she knew better than to respect a Marine.

"We won't let any old swabbie bother us, will we?"

Jurgen snarled—definitely Marine Corps. Swabbie was slang for a Navy sailor and a Marine always took offense at being lumped in with them no matter how much they belonged. Of course the swabbies took offense at having the Marines lumped with *them*. Too bad there weren't any Navy around so that she could get two for the price of one. Jurgen wouldn't be her boss, so appeasing him wasn't high on her to-do list.

At least she wouldn't need any of the protective bite gear working with Thor. With his stature, he was an explosives detection dog without also being an attack one.

"Where was he trained?" She stood back up to face the beast.

"Private outfit in Montana—some place called Henderson's Ranch. Didn't make their MWD program," his scoff said exactly what he thought the likelihood of any dog outfit in Montana being worthwhile. "They wanted us to try the little runt out."

She'd never heard of a training program in Montana. MWDs all came out of Lackland Air Force Base training. The Secret Service mostly trained their own and they all came from Vohne Liche Kennels in Indiana. Unless… Special Operations Forces dogs were trained by private contractors. She'd worked beside a Delta Force dog for a single month—he'd been incredible.

"Is he trained in English or German?" Most American MWDs were trained in German so that there was no confusion in case a command word happened to be part of a spoken sentence. It also made it harder for any random person on the battlefield to shout something that would confuse the dog.

"German according to his paperwork, but he won't listen to me much in either language."

Might as well give the diminutive Thor a few basic tests. A snap of her fingers and a slap on her thigh had the dog dropping into a smart "heel" position. No need to call out *Fuss*—*by my foot.*

"*Pass auf!*" Guard! She made a pistol with her thumb and forefinger and aimed it at Jurgen as she grabbed her forearm with her other hand—the military hand sign for enemy.

The little dog snarled at Jurgen sharply enough to have him backing out of the kennel. "Goddamn it!"

"*Ruhig.*" Quiet. Thor maintained his fierce posture but dropped the snarl.

"*Gute Hund.*" Good dog, Linda countered the command.

Thor looked up at her and wagged his tail happily. She tossed him a doggie treat, which he caught midair and crunched happily.

She didn't bother looking up at Jurgen as she knelt once more to check over the little dog. His scruffy fur was so soft that it tickled. Good strength in the jaw, enough to show he'd had bite training despite his size—perfect if she ever needed to take down a three-foot-tall terrorist. Legs said he was a jumper.

"Take your time, Hamlin. I've got nothing else to do with the rest of my goddamn day except babysit you and this mutt."

"Is the course set?"

"Sure. Take him out," Jurgen's snarl sounded almost as nasty as Thor's before he stalked off.

She stood and slapped a hand on her opposite shoulder.

Thor sprang aloft as if he was attached to springs and she caught him easily. He'd cleared well over double his own height. Definitely trained…and far easier to catch than seventy pounds of hyperactive Malinois.

She plopped him back down on the ground. On lead or off? She'd give him the benefit of the doubt and try off first to see what happened.

Linda zipped up her brand-new USSS jacket against the cold and led the way out of the kennel into the hard sunlight of the January morning. Snow had brushed the higher hills around the USSS James J. Rowley Training Center—which this close to Washington, DC, wasn't saying much—but was melting quickly. Scents wouldn't carry as well on the cool air, making it more of a challenge for Thor to locate the explosives. She didn't know where they were either. The course was a test for handler as well as dog.

Jurgen would be up in the observer turret looking for any excuse to mark down his newest team. Perhaps teasing him about being just a Marine hadn't been her best tactical choice. She sighed. At least she was consistent—she'd always been good at finding ways to piss people off before she could stop herself and consider the wisdom of doing so.

This test was the culmination of a crazy three months, so she'd forgive herself this time—something she also wasn't very good at.

In October she'd been out of the Army and unsure what to do next. Tucked in the packet with her DD 214 honorable discharge form had been a flyer on career opportunities with the US Secret Service dog team: *Be all your dog can be!* No one else being released from Fort Benning that day had received any kind of a job flyer at all that she'd seen, so she kept quiet about it.

She had to pass through DC on her way back to Vermont—her

parent's place. Burlington would work for, honestly, not very long at all, but she lacked anywhere else to go after a decade of service. So, she'd stopped off in DC to see what was up with that job flyer. Five interviews and three months to complete a standard six-month training course later—which was mostly a cakewalk after fighting with the US Rangers—she was on-board and this chill January day was her first chance with a dog. First chance to prove that she still had it. First chance to prove that she hadn't made a mistake in deciding that she'd seen enough bloodshed and war zones for one lifetime and leaving the Army.

The Start Here sign made it obvious where to begin, but she didn't dare hesitate to take in her surroundings past a quick glimpse. Jurgen's score would count a great deal toward where she and Thor were assigned in the future. Mostly likely on some field prep team, clearing the way for presidential visits.

As usual, hindsight informed her that harassing the lieutenant hadn't been an optimal strategy. A hindsight that had served her equally poorly with regular Army commanders before she'd finally hooked up with the Rangers—kowtowing to officers had never been one of her strengths.

Thankfully, the Special Operations Forces hadn't given a damn about anything except performance and *that* she could always deliver, since the day she'd been named the team captain for both soccer and volleyball. She was never popular, but both teams had made all-state her last two years in school.

The canine training course at James J. Rowley was a two-acre lot. A hard-packed path of tramped-down dirt led through the brown grass. It followed a predictable pattern from the gate to a junker car, over to tool shed, then a truck, and so on into a compressed version of an intersection in a small town. Beyond it ran an urban street of gray clapboard two- and three-story buildings and an eight-story office tower, all without windows. Clearly a playground for Secret Service training teams.

Her target was the town, so she blocked the city street out of her mind. Focus on the problem: two roads, twenty storefronts, six houses, vehicles, pedestrians.

It might look normal...normalish with its missing windows and no movement. It would be anything but. Stocked with fake IEDs, a bombmaker's stash, suicide cars, weapons caches, and dozens of other traps, all waiting for her and Thor to find. He had to be sensitive to hundreds of scents and it was her job to guide him so that he didn't miss the opportunity to find and evaluate each one.

There would be easy scents, from fertilizer and diesel fuel used so destructively in the 1995 Oklahoma City bombing, to almost as obvious TNT to the very difficult to detect C-4 plastic explosive.

Mannequins on the street carried grocery bags and briefcases. Some held fresh meat, a powerful smell demanding any dog's attention, but would count as a false lead if they went for it. On the job, an explosives detection dog wasn't supposed to care about anything except explosives. Other mannequins were wrapped in suicide vests loaded with Semtex or wearing knapsacks filled with package bombs made from Russian PVV-5A.

She spotted Jurgen stepping into a glassed-in observer turret atop the corner drugstore. Someone else was already there and watching.

She looked down once more at the ridiculous little dog and could only hope for the best.

"Thor?"

He looked up at her.

She pointed to the left, away from the beaten path.

"*Such!*" Find.

Thor sniffed left, then right. Then he headed forward quickly in the direction she pointed.

CLIVE ANDREWS SAT in the second-story window at the corner of

Main and First, the only two streets in town. Downstairs was a drugstore all rigged to explode, except there were no triggers and there was barely enough explosive to blow up a candy box.

Not that he'd know, but that's what Lieutenant Jurgen had promised him.

It didn't really matter if it was rigged to blow for real, because when Miss Watson—never Ms. or Mrs.—asked for a "favor," you did it. At least he did. Actually, he had yet to meet anyone else who knew her. Not that he'd asked around. She wasn't the sort of person one talked about with strangers, or even close friends. He'd bet even if they did, it would be in whispers. That's just what she was like.

So he'd traveled across town from the White House and into Maryland on a cold winter's morning, barely past a sunrise that did nothing to warm the day. Now he sat in an unheated glass icebox and watched a new officer run a test course he didn't begin to understand. Lieutenant Jurgen settled in beside him at a console with feeds from a dozen cameras and banks of switches.

While waiting, Clive had been fooling around with a sketch on a small pad of paper. The next State Dinner was in seven days. President Zachary Taylor had invited the leaders of Vietnam, Japan, and the Philippines to the White House for discussions about some Chinese islands. Or something like that, Clive hadn't really been paying attention to the details past the attendee list.

Instead, he was contemplating the dessert for such a dinner that would surprise, perhaps delight, as well as being an icebreaker for future discussions. Being the chocolatier for the White House was the most exciting job he'd ever had. Every challenge was fresh and new, like the first strawberry of each year.

This one would be elegant. January was a little early, it would be better if it was spring, but that wasn't crucial. A large half-egg shape of paper-thin white chocolate filled with a mousse—white chocolate? No, nor a dark chocolate. Instead, a milk chocolate mousse but rich with flavor, perhaps bourbon.

Then mold the dark chocolate to top it with a filigree bird, wings spread in half flight, ready to soar upward. A crane perhaps? He made a note to check with the protocol office to make sure that he wouldn't be offending some leader without knowing it.

"Never underestimate the power of a good dessert," he mumbled one of Jacques Torres' favorite admonitions. This was going to work very nicely.

"What's that?" Jurgen grunted out without looking up.

"Just talking to myself."

Which earned him a dismissive grunt, as if he was unworthy of the agent's attention. It wouldn't surprise him. Clive was not trained like a Secret Service officer. His skills lay in his palate and his fingers for shaping the very finest chocolate work. He knew his big frame and good looks said easy-going and, while his size wasn't quite to oaf, people always assumed he was just a big and clumsy guy.

Clive often felt defensive about being a chocolatier when he was so dismissed out of hand. He had spent years learning his skills. And to be invited to join the White House kitchen...well, he couldn't think of a higher accolade. The fact that his father would agree with Jurgen didn't help matters. However, Lieutenant Jurgen didn't look like the sort of man to risk upsetting.

His own father had been a quiet, drunken merchant marine who rarely spoke when he was ashore—except for grumblings about his only child's lame excuse for a choice of profession. The one blessing of having Nic Andrews as a father was how much of Clive's life the man had spent at sea. In between, Clive and his mother had lived together in Redwood City very quietly and with some small degree of content. Their apartment had a view of the brilliant colors of the Cargill Salt Flats of San Francisco Bay. He often used their colors in his chocolates.

"They're starting." It was clear by his tone that Jurgen could break Clive over his knee like a piece of sugar work despite

Clive's size and would be glad to demonstrate at the least provocation.

"Oh, thanks," seemed to be an acceptable response.

A "you're welcome" grunt sounded softly.

Miss Watson had told him to watch, so he closed his notepad and tucked it in his shirt pocket.

"Any suggestions on what I'm looking for?" Miss Watson had *not* been clear on that point. He looked down at the new officer and the small dog entering the far end of the course. He picked up a pair of binoculars from the window ledge but the dog was still small, barely reaching the officer's knees.

He scanned upward.

A woman. For some reason he hadn't expected that. Of course with the silly little dog, that somehow fit. However, officer or not, the woman offered a great deal to be looking at. Five-seven or eight. Medium chocolate brunette, about a fifty percent cocoa, with a nicely tempered shine like a fine ganache. It fell in a natural flow down to her shoulders, slightly ragged rather than in some DC socialite perfect coif. A thin face without being gaunt. Perhaps intense would be a better word.

Her jacket hid her shape, but she wore no hat or gloves despite the cold. Tan khakis hinted at nice legs. Army boots declared definitely not DC socialite.

"Well, for one thing, she's not following the damned course," Jurgen sounded puzzled.

"Is that a bad thing?" Clive could see the worn track and that they definitely weren't on it.

Jurgen made a sound that was neither yes or no.

"What's her name?"

"Linda with Thor," as if it was a single name.

Clive couldn't stop the laugh. "*That* scruffy little mutt is named Thor?"

Jurgen's grin would look appropriately nasty to be carved into the flesh of a Halloween pumpkin.

The woman had transformed once she started the course. Pretty and intent had transformed to focused to the point of lethal. She moved with all the efficiency of a fine-honed knife blade. Maybe she was Thor and the dog was Linda.

With a series of hand signs—Linda's mouth rarely moved though he did spend some time watching it—she directed the dog along a storefront. When she disappeared inside, he turned to watch the camera feeds on Jurgen's console.

"It isn't just the dog," Jurgen volunteered. "The dog has the nose, but the handler guides the dog to make sure no area is missed. Neither one can do it alone. Hundred percent a team effort."

Inside what might have been a real estate or travel agency, the dog sat abruptly and looked back at Linda. The officer stuck a red Post-it on one of the desk drawers.

"PETN. Very hard to find. Under half of the dog teams find that one," Jurgen didn't sound pleased. Maybe he was one of those people who was only happy when someone was suffering. Clive had worked for more than one chef like that.

"Linda with Thor"—or "Thor with Linda," he wasn't going to commit on that one yet despite Jurgen's evil grin—were on the move again.

Just as they stepped out of the office, Jurgen flipped a switch on his console.

Clive jumped as the blast of sirens sounded from a police car parked at the curb, even though they were muffled by distance and the observer station's windows.

It must have been painfully loud right next to the car, but Linda and Thor both merely looked at the wailing vehicle, sniffed their way around it, then continued along the street.

For an hour they left behind a trail of red Post-its and for the most part ignored sirens, gunfire, and other distractions. Once an actual explosion spattered them with dirt. For that, Linda had wrapped her arms around the dog and huddled in a bookstore doorway with her back turned toward the worst of it. Moments later they were back at their task.

Clive could look down in wonder. She'd positioned herself so that if the explosion had been lethal, rather than merely a training distraction, she'd have given her life to save her dog. Maybe the guys on the Presidential Protection Detail really would step in front of the bullet if given the chance. Would he himself step in the line of a rogue chocolate shard? Perhaps, but only because that didn't sound terribly threatening.

When they reached the end of the course, they stopped in the center of the intersection. From a small pack, she pulled out a fold-up bowl and poured some water into it for Thor before drinking herself. Then a doggie treat. Nothing for the handler.

With a tip of his head, Jurgen indicated that Clive should follow him down.

As they stepped out onto the street themselves, she was tossing a bulbous Kong toy for Thor. He'd once more turned into the dog most likely to belong at a little girl's tea party, eating all of the cookies whenever the hostess wasn't looking.

"You missed two," Jurgen snapped out his form of a polite greeting, not bothering to look at his clipboard.

Linda flinched as if she'd been slapped and her shoulders sagged.

But Clive had learned some things about Jurgen's expressions: there was a sourness there like bitter chocolate. "What's been your best score by any other team?"

"Five misses," Jurgen's scowl now included him since Clive had just spoiled his fun.

Linda still didn't look any happier. That told him a lot about her—this was one seriously driven woman. Anything less than perfect was a hundred percent failure. Which he supposed was true when your job was to make sure that no one blew up the President.

At that moment Thor stopped playing with his toy, trotted up to Jurgen's feet, circled him once, and sat abruptly with his nose aimed at one of the lieutenant's shoes.

"Damn it," he growled. "Okay, that makes one miss."

"Let me guess," Clive could get to enjoy this after all. "The observer's station also has an explosive." Then his breath caught in his throat. He wouldn't put it past Jurgen to have him sitting on an explosive the whole time he'd been in the observer's chair.

JURGEN'S EXPRESSION said it all.

"Of course," Linda couldn't believe she'd missed it. "It is always the person and place you least suspect that gets by you." *That* was certainly never going to happen again.

She was furious with herself for missing that but wasn't going to show any weakness. It was one of the great traps of serving in the military. If a woman showed the least weakness, she'd forever be tagged as unable to perform. If a guy showed ten times as much, he'd be tagged as being tired and probably told he'd done a good job. The military had taught her how to hide *anything* she was actually feeling—often until she barely felt it herself.

It was even more galling that some stranger had to be the one to point it out. He didn't sound or act like Secret Service, making it even worse.

"Usually takes a new dog-handler team weeks of hard work to get even close to that kind of performance. Fine!" Jurgen's tone said it was anything but. He yanked a sheet from his clipboard, scrawled a signature, and handed it across. "Oh eight hundred tomorrow. Report to Captain Carl Baxter at the USSS office in the West Wing of the White House. Take that damn dog with you. I've got a meeting to get to." Then he stalked off. A trumped-up meeting, because earlier he'd said he had all day.

Linda could only look down at Thor in amazement. She squatted down and gave him a big scritch. It wasn't Thor's fault that she'd screwed up and not led him into the control center to sniff around and she had to make sure that he knew that. She'd never before worked with such a well-trained dog. He flopped onto his back and presented his belly. As she rubbed it, his back leg began kicking spasmodically in joy.

"You did so good, Thor. You are such a good doggie!" She used that ridiculous high-pitched voice that so many dog trainers used. She was long past being embarrassed by it. Mostly. She couldn't care less about Jurgen, but something about the other man who'd stayed behind made her less sure.

"Maybe I should leave you two alone." He had a nice deep voice, befitting his large frame.

Linda glanced up at him. Her automatic profiling assessment kicked in: Caucasian male, closecut dark hair, dark eyes, built big like a wrestler—enough so that he'd look heavy if he wasn't six-four. Instead he looked like the guy most likely to wrap you up in a friendly bear hug, which would force her to flatten him if he tried. His standout feature was powerful hands well marked with small cuts and burns. That and an amazing smile, which lit up his whole face. He wore a fleece jacket over a maroon turtleneck and a knit scarf in a blocky pattern of brilliant colors that made his brown eyes even warmer.

"Hi," his pleasant tone not the least diminished by her own silence, which was now growing awkward.

Thor had rolled to his feet, sniffed around the man, then looked up at him wagging his short tail.

He knelt down and reached out to scratch the dog's ear.

She snapped her fingers to get Thor's attention and made the hand sign for "enemy" as a test.

He looked up at her in surprise as if she'd lost her mind.

She sighed and whispered, "*Spiel.*" *Play.* The dog could do what he wanted.

He nosed out and slipped his head under the stranger's half-extended hand. Without a moment's hesitation, the man began to rub the offered ear. Easy for the dog.

Not so easy for her. Well, she had to start somewhere and he looked kindly enough.

"Nice scarf."

He looked down at his chest. "Oh, this one. Thanks. My mom knit it for me last Christmas. It's the colors of home."

"Where did you grow up, in a kaleidoscope?"

"Almost. South of San Francisco there are these huge salt flats that turn wild colors as their salinity increases. This is the last scarf she ever knit for me. I made one of cherry blossom colors for her that same year." His smile was wistful, which was more than she'd ever feel if her mom died.

"You knit?" She couldn't imagine how with those big hands of his.

"Doesn't everyone?" But his smile said that rather than an actual expectation, it was some form of humor—not one of her strengths. It was getting strange, not knowing if he was someone to salute or not, so she held out a hand.

"Sergeant Linda Hamlin. New to the Secret Service—as of today, I suppose."

"Clive Andrews," which still didn't tell her who he was. He reached up from where he still squatted by Thor. His hand was warm—her fingers were freezing—and as powerful as it looked. His massive hand completely enveloped hers. That's when she realized that he wasn't merely big, he was immensely strong. If he was trained, she might have trouble taking him down—though she'd learned more than a few dirty tricks fending off unwanted attentions in her decade of service.

There was an easy roll to his voice that hinted at Scottish, overlaid with a soft American accent that she couldn't pin down— which must be San Francisco. It made him sound as much of a mutt as Thor.

"Not *Agent* Hamlin?"

14

"*Special Agent* is separate from the Uniformed Division. The canine teams are UD; we use ranks."

"Oh."

Great way to build a friendship—her first potential one outside of the military in a decade—by correcting him. It did tell her that he wasn't Secret Service or he'd have known that. Which raised the question of what he was doing on their secure base.

"And this is a White House patrol dog?" He rubbed under Thor's chin.

She looked down at Thor's shaggy appearance. Despite his exceptional performance, it was clear that she was going to be endlessly harassed about him. She sighed and changed the subject.

"And you are...?" Best way to appease a man, talk about *him*.

"The White House chocolatier." His cheery wince said that he too was expecting a certain dismissive reaction.

When she didn't take the bait, he merely acknowledged it with a shrug.

Again the silence was stretching... "Is there a reason a chocolatier is here at James J. Rowley Training Center?"

This time the shrug looked a little awkward as he rose back to standing, much to Thor's dismay.

She was an expert on reading a dog's body language. Men were a mystery to her. Well, except for a few obvious nonverbal messages that she had made it a rule to ignore. But she wasn't getting those from Clive the Chocolatier.

"Grown men actually make their living with chocolate?"

That earned her another of his dazzling smiles, "Only the lucky ones."

"Chocolate was never a big motivator for me."

He slapped a hand on his heart and staggered backward as if she'd knifed him with her Benchmade Triage foldable. "You have set me a challenge, madam. I shall expect you to visit the White House Chocolate Shop at your first convenience so that I may convince you otherwise."

"The White House has a chocolate *shop?* Like where you buy chocolate?" She was definitely back in civilian land. The places she'd been operating, a chow tent was a luxury and a mess hall mostly a distant dream.

He sighed and hung his head as if she was a hopeless case, which wouldn't surprise her for a moment. But then he smiled down at her again, as cheerful as ever. He and Thor were apparently two of a kind.

"Actually, in the world of chocolate, a chocolate shop can be either a place of sale or a kitchen. Mine is a actually a chocolate kitchen. We just call it a shop."

"Okay. Sure. Whatever. I'll look you up if I get there." A chill breeze flapped the piece of paper directing her to report at the White House tomorrow and made her shiver. "Okay, *when* I get there."

Clive cast off his fooling around. His friendliness actually made her feel warm despite the freezing temperature. She really needed to get some gloves. Did he know how powerful that smile was on his handsome features?

Her jerk-o-meter wasn't twitching either, which was unusual.

Then, of all unlikely things, he bowed deeply—once to her and once to Thor, the second bow accompanied by a brief head pat—before turning and heading for the parking lot.

A nice guy. One who remembered her dog. She didn't like being charmed by any creature with less than four legs, but he'd somehow managed it.

CHAPTER TWO

"*And?*"

Clive wondered how anyone could pack so many emotions into such an innocuous word: inquiry, curiosity, impatience, and a touch of someone busy working on a jigsaw puzzle in which he himself was but one of the smaller pieces. Not the most comfortable feeling.

That it was also Miss Watson's form of a greeting only made it all the stranger. As if they were in the middle of a conversation that he'd already missed the start of and would never catch back up with as it raced away from him.

He always felt like a cave explorer whenever he came down here.

Her office was a tiny space deep in the White House Residence's lowest subbasement. It was two stories below the kitchen and his chocolate shop, directly beneath the dishwashing room. The latter was proven by the nest of drain piping that covered the ceiling of her office. Any conversation here was punctuated by a succession of gurgles from dishwashers flushing away the remains of meals, ranging from the President's private dinners to massive state banquets.

The walls were old brick that probably dated back to the massive Truman renovation. They were lined with packed-solid bookshelves. He'd never been able to make sense of the titles. Even an eclectic reader was unlikely to cover such a range of interests: religious texts, English law, German something or other (not one of his languages, not that he actually had any other than mostly forgotten high school French only slightly enhanced while apprenticed to the great Jacques Torres in New York), contemporary thrillers, dictionaries in a variety of languages...

As an excuse to look somewhere other than her steel blue eyes, he inspected her collection of curious artifacts—some of which he wondered how Miss Watson had gotten past White House security. Fierce knives and strange-looking rifles that were like none he'd ever seen being carried by the Secret Service or the military. Some of them looked like they'd be more appropriate in a spy movie than in real life.

High on one wall, with its own tiny spotlight as if it was a place of honor, a tattered wool scarf hung pressed in a glass frame, faded almost a uniform gray with hard usage. The sloppy knitting followed no discernable pattern. There were even holes that he could tell had been dropped stitches that had expanded with age. He'd never found the nerve to ask about it and, he thought about it a moment, today wasn't going to be the day he braved her daunting expression.

The office looked as if not even a single dust mote had been changed since his first visit here three months ago.

It had been a lovely day in October, one of the most beautiful months in DC. He'd found a note. Not a text or an e-mail, a handwritten note in a flowing black ink script. The problem was that it had been locked inside his personal recipe file box—to which he knew for a fact he had the only key.

"Come see me. Residence, Subbasement Two, Room 043." Nothing more. The paper had begun to dissolve just from the moisture on his fingers. He dropped it in the sink and it dissolved completely in the moisture accumulated there.

He'd only been called to her twice since and always left more puzzled than when he arrived. Everything about the room made the small, gray-haired woman who sat behind the battered steel desk seem all the more daunting and mysterious.

He tried not to fidget and totally failed. "Sergeant Linda Hamlin's score on the course was apparently exceptional. She—"

"I have them here," Miss Watson rested her hand on a slim file.

"Then why did you send me out to—"

"Tell me what isn't in the file."

Protesting that he didn't know what *was* included in the file didn't seem like a path that would lead anywhere good, so he abandoned it untested.

Clive wished that Miss Watson had actual guest chairs—not that the office was big enough to accommodate them. Instead, she had a single, four-legged wooden stool on which one of the legs was a half inch short. Sitting on it, he always felt out of balance... and kept checking his head to see if he should be wearing a dunce cap like the bad boy in the corner. It was also short enough that even with his stature he was barely eye-to-eye with her across the desk.

He looked at her again. Penetrating blue eyes. Silver hair back in a 1950s bun. She wore a hand-knit cable cardigan adorned only by a small bronze broach in the form of an oak leaf. She had an intricately patterned sock of gray, pale orange, and brown wool half completed on the corner of her desk. It was a Fair Isle pattern he'd learned at his mother's knee. He'd rather talk knitting than what he didn't know about Linda and Thor—but the thin needles caught the low desk light brightly, making them appear dangerous, as if they were weapons of war rather than of wool.

He'd never raised the subject of knitting with her on any of the four occasions she'd had reason to call him to her office. And he wasn't brave enough to this time either.

"Linda and Thor, a rather silly-looking little dog, moved about the course as if they were a single being connected by gesture and tone. They were more cohesive than most restaurants' menu plans, though Lieutenant Jurgen said it was their first meeting. There was a well-trodden path leading into the test area that they *didn't* follow. Linda led them onto a path of her own choosing instead."

"They see no boundaries." Miss Watson typically gave him the impression that he was only one of a myriad of more important topics she was contemplating. He now had her full attention and wished he didn't—it was rather daunting.

He tried to think of what else might not be in a performance report by Lieutenant Jurgen.

Linda's lovely face, flowing hair, and cautious eyes came to mind. Also, how hard it had been not to reach for her fine hand again as he left. He'd wanted to hold it again, however briefly, and that seemed a little creepy so he'd done his best courtly bow instead.

"During the course, there was a mock explosion that spattered them with dirt. Linda put Thor's life ahead of her own, shielding the dog with her own body. She did it so fast that I never saw it happen."

"You like her," Miss Watson made it a flat statement.

"Linda offers a lot to be admired."

Miss Watson brushed that aside with a flick of her ringless fingers. "You like her."

He grimaced. At which Miss Watson smiled like a benevolent grandmother rather than a scary old lady in the White House subbasement who was never discussed on the floors above. Did the politicians orbited through and mingled in the Residence even know she was down here?

"It is not mindreading. Your voice and expression would give you away. Your automatic use of her first name as well. Yes," Miss Watson gazed up at the waste pipes that formed her ceiling but appeared to be looking up through the two subbasements and the four stories of the Residence, right up to the Delta Force snipers permanently stationed on the roof. "Yes, I shall have to arrange to meet her."

"She promised to come by my chocolate shop."

Miss Watson tipped her head down to look at him as if she was glaring over the rims of her reading glasses, except she didn't wear any.

"Uh…"

She waited.

"Perhaps I'd best be going."

"Perhaps," her tone was drier and grittier than under-conched cocoa. "But before you depart, I would ask you to consider one question. What boundaries stop you, Mr. Andrews?" Then she picked up her knitting and he knew he was summarily dismissed.

He got out while the getting was good.

CHAPTER THREE

*T*hor eyed her strangely.

"Give me a break." Linda's feet were riveted to the sidewalk. But there was no explaining to a dog that the broad green lawn and white stone building on the other side of the stout fence was anything more than a giant park specially designed for dogs to go pee in.

Even as she stood there, gawking through the black iron fence at the White House like any other tourist, a USSS dog team came working along the sidewalk. Before she could see their dog, it was easy to spot the handler: six feet of strapping immensely fit male in the black uniform and jacket of the Uniformed Division. Dark sunglasses despite the recent sunrise.

She envied the thin leather gloves protecting his hands. She'd found a battered pair of fingerless shooter's gloves in her gear, but they didn't keep her hands much warmer. Her last duties in Africa and Fort Benning, Georgia, hadn't called for anything more. DC's bitter winter was contending with fall evenings in Vermont and she'd forgotten how cold those were.

But rather than a proud German shepherd parting the crowd like a plowshare, a handsome springer spaniel nosed his way out of the crowd, swinging a little left and right to check the air swirled about by the few early morning joggers. It was still too early on a chilly morning for tourists and protestors to flock to the White House fence, but the dog team was already on duty.

The handsome dog handler stopped in front of her wearing a big smile.

"First day? I know the look. Still feels that way every time I look at the place." He turned to his dog. *"Gute Hund."* The dog immediately relaxed its vigilance and came over to meet Thor.

"Uh, yeah. Guess so." Linda wondered if she could sound any lamer.

"Malcolm," he nodded toward the spaniel presently trading butt sniffs with Thor. "I'm Jim." Maybe he was okay despite his looks—it took a true dog handler to introduce his animal first.

"Thor. I'm Linda," and she wasn't going to get tagged with being lame. "One word about his name and you'll find yourself on your ass real fast."

Jim held up his warmly gloved hands palm out.

"Just sayin'," she put on her nicest tone.

"Hey, we floppy-eareds gotta stick together," again the unexpected genuineness of his smile. "Though Thor is kinda the extreme example I've seen."

"Floppy-eareds?"

"Friendly dogs. PSCO—Personnel Screening Canines Open Area. You'll see. The Emergency Response Team and the other behind-the-scenes dogs, they get the big muscle. We get the total sweethearts," the last he spoke in happy dog, squeaky pitch to Malcolm, who thumped his short tail against Jim's leg.

It made her like him even better—again the sign of a true dog handler. Maybe the world wasn't all made up of Jerk Jurgens. Or handsome chocolatiers.

"Well, gotta go. We got bad guys to catch. Go see the captain, he'll get you off on the right foot. See ya down the fence line. Later, Thor. *Such,*" he told Malcolm, who instantly headed forward into the thickening morning crowd along the fence line. Jim waved at her and moved off. She half wondered if he even remembered her name. Then she caught him glancing back…and she knew the timing: calculated to let him check her out, then glancing away fast when he knew he'd been caught.

Fine. Whatever.

A second UD officer separated from the crowd and followed Jim and Malcolm. He didn't have a dog; instead he had an AR-15 assault rifle slung across his chest. Teams of two.

She headed to the gate and showed her temporary ID to the guard inside the entrance's security hut. He scanned it, looking back and forth between her and the screen a couple of times before returning it. Then he waved her toward the metal scanner and she just rolled her eyes at him.

"What?"

"Collar, leash, handcuffs, sidearm, utility knife, taser, spare magazines…should I keep going?"

He leaned forward and looked down over the counter. "Oh. Didn't see your dog down there."

She held up the badge again, which said Secret Service K-9 on it rather than pulling out a baton and cracking him smartly on the head. She *was* learning patience.

"Right. Okay. But that's a temporary. Can't let you on the grounds while armed without an escort." Before she could think what to say, he was on the phone. It only took a moment. "You're expected. You can go through, but wait by the door."

She walked through the metal detector, which squealed in several nasty tones but, as no one shot her, she kept moving. She walked down a short hallway watched over by an attentive looking agent behind a tall counter made of louvered metal.

Thor swung aside and came to a halt as he sniffed at the screening.

"You're screwing up my job," the agent grumbled.

Linda tried to figure out how.

Thor was wagging his tail. The same way he had when he'd met Malcolm the springer spaniel along the fence line.

Then she felt it and looked up. Warmth! She raised her hand, the one not holding Thor's leash, closer to the source. It felt so good. A fan was blowing a slow waft of warm air down over her. It was…oh! Just enough to drive the air down and through the louvers along the counter. An EDT—Explosives Detection Team —dog would be on the other side of the louver beside the disgruntled agent.

"Tell him that Thor says hello."

"She," the agent looked down at his own dog, out of sight behind the counter, with a growl deep in his throat.

And apparently some of the White House handlers *were* closely related to Jerk Jurgens.

Linda tapped her thigh and led Thor out of the entry screening hut. Outside the air was fresh and the sun bright. She didn't mind the cold as much as she had earlier. Until she tucked her fingertips under opposite armpits and realized they were chilled to the bone.

Captain Baxter—by his shield and name badge—came up to her and held out a hand. "Sergeant Linda Hamlin. That like the Pied Piper of Hamelin or like Linda Hamilton in *Terminator?*" Naming her for the movie star was not one of her mother's kinder acts—not that her mother was known for that particular trait.

"Neither, sir." She *had* been named for Linda Hamilton, but for her role in *Beauty and the Beast* so Linda could properly deny any association with *Terminator.* An unfortunate similarity in looks that she'd never been able to live down made it even worse. She managed not to clench her jaw, but considered seeing just what attack skills *had* been taught to Thor.

The captain continued blithely on as he guided her toward the West Entrance to the White House, unaware of just how close she'd come to unleashing some wholly inappropriate response.

"So, Jurgen finally found someone willing to give the little scruff ball a chance."

"Yes, sir."

"Assessment?" He asked it just a little too casually. Was he messing with her? Or did he know things she didn't and this was some sort of test?

"His acuity is exceptional. Good-natured, yet deeply trained to the handler-dog bond. Whoever trained him I suspect is highly qualified. Though I understand he's the first dog from a new kennel."

"Stan Corman. Navy SEAL, retired." The captain made a chopping motion with one hand against the biceps of his other arm. "Lost his dog and his arm at the same time. The two of them saved my life a couple years before that. Got out while I was still in one piece and came on board here. He landed at some place in nowhere Montana named Henderson's Ranch. I owe the man a chance and then some."

So, she'd done something right in accepting Thor. Wouldn't that just tick off Lieutenant Jurgen.

Through the foyer, again the badges cleared by security, and down a long hall crowded with rushing people.

Her nerves, which had bolted her to the sidewalk outside the fence line, blew up so high that she was amazed the White House roof didn't go with them. She was inside the bubble of the Commander-in-Chief. To her right were the doors to the Situation Room where any number of her last ten years' missions had been authorized. The Navy Mess.

While she gawked, the Vice President strode in chatting with the White House Chief of Staff as if it was a normal, everyday occurrence. She was *so* out of her depth. Only Thor's light pull on his leash kept her moving forward at all.

At the far end of the hall, Captain Baxter led her through a door labeled United States Secret Service. This at least felt familiar from her training. The craziness on the other side of the door? She'd be perfectly happy to never cross the fence line again. She and Thor would patrol the streets, and the people in here she'd just leave to do whatever people in here did.

The Secret Service Ready Room was packed with desks along the walls—about half of them occupied. At one end was a briefing area that could hold twenty or so agents, at the other were two glassed-in offices barely big enough to hold a desk and a chair each.

In one sat an agent with light brown, close-cropped hair. He was a few inches shorter than Clive and about half his size… Now why was she thinking about the chocolatier? She shook her head to clear it. The agent punched at a keyboard as if he was trying to kill it. The sign beside his office door didn't even bear a name, just PPD—Presidential Protection Detail.

Baxter led her into the other office marked UD—Uniformed Division.

He jabbed a finger at the lone chair as he closed the door.

She sat. Thor lay down at her feet.

Dropping into his own chair, Baxter slapped a hand on a file thick enough to be her entire personnel file and then some.

"All of this true?"

"Not having read it, sir, I wouldn't know."

"Commendations coming out of your goddamn ears, Sergeant. If *you* brought this to me, I'd have chucked it in the trash because I'd know one thing for certain—that you were a lying suck-up, forging shit to get near the President."

"Sir." Linda didn't know what else to say. She hadn't been some superstar, just a woman trying to play it dead clean in a man's world.

"Number of female dog handlers qualified to fight with the 75th Rangers: one. Number of female dog handlers in any branch of the military with not one, not two, but three medals for valor including a Bronze Star—all with the V for "in combat" on all three: one. Clearance Top Secret with SCI and SAP."

And Linda hoped that she'd never see another thing like it. Sensitive Compartmented Information and Special Access Programs information was always a nightmare.

"Seventeen of your actions over the last five years are redacted so that even I can't tell what the hell you were doing. You care to tell me?"

"No, sir." She wasn't at liberty to do so, no matter what his clearance.

"Good girl."

Okay, not girl. Not even woman. Soldier! Training in silence was all that let her keep the comment inside. Besides, only seventeen of her missions redacted? That meant that a number of her missions were so highly classified that they weren't in her file at all—at least not the version made available to the Secret Service.

"What in the name of all that's holy and the US Army are you doing in my office?"

"Reporting for duty?" What kind of a trick question was that?

Baxter stared at the closed file for a long moment before looking back at her. "Draw me a map, Hamlin. US Rangers to US Secret Service. How did you get here?"

"There was a flyer in my DD 214 discharge packet. USSS K-9 team recruiting. *Be all your dog can be.* Sounded like me."

He barked a short laugh. "I like it. But we don't do that. We don't have flyers."

"Well, someone put it there. Looked better than going back to Vermont." Throwing herself naked into the Potomac in January looked better than that.

Baxter harrumphed. Then scowled at Thor, who had lain down at her feet.

"Damned if I know what to make of it. We get good men applying for this job, a lot of them."

He didn't emphasize *men,* so she kept her thoughts to herself.

"Most of them straight out of college with some nutso ideas

about glory. Takes forever to straighten them out and some we never do. That's not you."

"That's not me," Linda agreed.

"A woman with a decade of service and half of it with the 75th Rangers," he mused to himself. "I'll be damned." Without further comment, Baxter leaned over his desk and slapped a hand against the wall.

While they were waiting for whatever response, he dug a bright-brass USSS Uniformed Division badge out of his pocket and tossed it to her. She pinned it to her uniform's left lapel, taking only a moment to rub her thumb over the embossed image of the White House and the small blue plaque at the bottom with "Sergeant" etched into it.

A moment after she had it affixed, the door opened and the agent from the PPD office next door stepped in and closed the door behind him.

"This her?"

Baxter just nodded.

Her what? Linda didn't have time to be more than puzzled by the remark.

"Hello. I'm Harvey Lieber, Senior Special Agent in charge of President Zachary Thomas' protection detail."

"Linda Hamlin," she'd have stood if there was room, but there wasn't.

"Out of the friggin' blue," Baxter grumbled.

"And?"

Baxter eyed her. "Jurgen doesn't give anyone top marks. I keep him out at Rowley to scare the ego out of all the rookies, even the agents back for refresher training who are getting too cocky. He gave them to her, though. I told you about Stan Corman sending me a dog."

"That?" Lieber looked down at Thor, who began batting a front paw in his sleep as if chasing a rabbit.

Linda hoped it was a little field bunny, because he wasn't all that much bigger than a jackrabbit.

"That," Baxter agreed.

"Should do nicely."

Linda twisted around to get a better look at him, but it didn't tell her anything.

"Can you be presentable?" Agent Lieber looked down at her.

She waved a hand at herself. This was how she came. In uniform with her hair and teeth brushed.

"I mean in a high-end social crowd. Not asking if you're pretty —that's obvious and irrelevant, though not a bad thing in this situation. Asking if you know how to behave."

"My mother wishes I did." Mom had always been pushing her into the political events in Montpelier, Vermont—as if it was Albany, New York, or some other much larger and more important state's capital. Was she supposed to become a conniving politician like her mother, whose ethics had nothing to do with reality and everything to do with partisan stratagems and counterattacks? Or was she supposed to become like her father, teaching at University of Vermont, Burlington, because of all the coeds who flocked to handsome poli-sci professors whenever his wife was off to Montpelier?

"Which means you know how, you just hate it. Couldn't care. Your call, Baxter. First Family flies out in an hour, I can't deal with this right now." And just that fast he was gone.

"What the hell?"

Baxter raised his eyebrows.

"Sir."

CLIVE WENT through his morning routine on autopilot.

The Chocolate Shop was so small that it was a good thing there was a coat closet between it and the main kitchen. The twenty-foot-square room was immaculate and, with all of the counters and equipment, left little space for anything extraneous like his coat.

The conching machine ground happily away in the corner, smoothing and heating the chocolate to uniformly distribute the cocoa butter throughout. It's background hum always made him feel as if everything was okay. The dark chocolate required three days of conching. It had taken some real magic to squeeze the machine into his tiny kitchen, but the results were absolutely worth it.

He studied several of the sketches he'd taped on the face of the spice cabinet. He peeled away the chocolate cake he'd made for Christmas and the white chocolate and strawberry streusel from New Year's Eve. He liked to think of it as clearing the decks for what came next. Many other surfaces had neat rows of images that inspired him, but the spice cabinet was only for the actual desserts he was going to make and he never repeated.

He unlocked the pantry and main chocolate storage cabinet that kept everything at fifty degrees. His supplies were all in place.

A peek inside his smaller storage cabinet, which he left at sixty degrees and never locked, said that the overnight damage hadn't been too severe. He made a point of leaving "extra" confections there, which were frequently raided when the staff had to work late. He made a mental note to keep the level of truffles a little higher and form the chocolate bars smaller. Apparently people felt too guilty taking the larger chocolate bars when raiding his kitchen. He took a few minutes with a hot knife to cut them neatly into halves and thirds. He lay a small bet with himself as to how many would survive another night.

Of course whenever Clive caught a "thief," he took deep umbrage and soundly berated the individual—it was the only time he unleashed his father's brogue. "An' what makes ye think that ye deserve such *snashters,* you blaggard?" And the like. Lasses, of course, were treated more kindly. It came out half drunken-Scot and half pirate-captain—all in good fun.

The "public" cabinet was a good testing method for new creations. He'd leave several options, and often discovered that one had been completely cleared out and another barely touched. Last night had been an even fifty-fifty, so nothing new to learn there. He found that disappointing, he'd rather thought his lavender-brushed honey truffles would be more popular than the vanilla-cream-filled extra-dark bonbon.

"Back to the drawing board, lad."

Which reminded him of yesterday's sketch. Drawn, but now he'd have to write out the process of execution.

He took his time heating milk to two hundred degrees, rinsing his favorite mug under the boiling-water tap to bring it up to temperature, and then mixing in his homemade cocoa powder. He sipped it, but it wasn't quite right. Christmas was recently gone— the holiday madness that wracked the White House kitchens every year had subsided—but it was too abrupt. He fished a whole nutmeg out of the pantry and used a rasp to grate a little over his mug. A pinch of allspice and a quick stir. He let it steep for a minute or two to blend properly, then tasted it again.

Yes, just a little nostalgia after the holidays to soften the blow of descent from the madness of the holidays into the bland, unending stretch of January. Nothing ever happened in January... except for mesmerizing dog trainers.

He sat at the marble counter with his cocoa and his notepad, finally allowing himself to flip to the sketch he'd made yesterday while out at the James J. Rowley facility. He studied it carefully. It was pretty enough—a white chocolate, half eggshell with jagged edges, filled with a bourbon mousse and crowned with fanciful dark chocolate work.

Something wasn't right there. At least not yet. Perhaps because the crane also looked like a stork and neither the President nor the Vice President had reproduced yet. That created a mixed message that he wasn't wholly comfortable with. A bluebird perhaps? Did Southeast Asians believe in the bluebird of happiness?

Something more bothered him, but he was having trouble pinning it down.

Vietnam, Japan, and the Philippines. The only thing their flags had in common was the color red. Hard to play off that.

Using Marou chocolate from Lam Dong province might please the Vietnamese delegation, but might well insult the others for perceived favoritism. While the Philippine chocolatiers were doing well, only Kablon and Malagos came close to the same standard. And Japan didn't make chocolate at all. Regrettably, to avoid offense, he'd have to go South American or African. But that still didn't solve the lack of a Japanese element.

The dessert felt almost old hat—three different grades of chocolate to make...

No. He wanted something...

The words were eluding him. He knew from experience that only when he found the right words could he then design the confection.

He studied the sketch again. It was pretty enough, but it was lacking in meaning.

He crumpled up the page and tossed it away. Yesterday it would have been good enough, but not today.

Clive doodled on the corner of the next page while he contemplated what had changed. It wasn't merely enough to achieve, he wanted to excel. Something had shifted in his understanding of what he did.

Life was like that, perceptions growing and changing in fits and starts, and he'd come to anticipate their arrival. By the time he understood that he was a chocolatier, he had already graduated from the CIA—the Culinary Institute of America—and slaved for four years under the eagle eye of two different masters, one in Chicago and another in LA before finally going to work for the great Jacques Torres in Manhattan. He sipped his hot cocoa again after raising it in a toast to the signed photograph of Torres and himself on the wall.

The invitation to the White House had shocked Clive until he had looked back at his steady climb up the ranks of the nation's dessert kitchens post-Torres: the Beverly Wilshire in LA, The Plaza in New York, The Greenbriar...

Only in retrospect did his life ever make sense.

He was less certain about what had changed last night, though something definitely had. He was no longer content with a design that just yesterday he would have happily created and he knew would have been well received.

Whatever the seed of the change, he could see more clearly now. It was not enough for his dessert to be pretty and a topic of conversation. It had to have meaning. It had to have...purpose.

There! That was the problem. He knew almost nothing about the purpose of the dinner he was designing for.

He tapped his pen on the page. Who to ask? The kitchen team wouldn't know any more than he did. Chef Klaus was not exactly an elevated thinker. An elevated chef? Absolutely. But thinking wasn't an ingredient he used very often.

Clive sipped at his cocoa for inspiration, but only found an unpleasantly lukewarm concoction that had a little too much allspice in it.

Miss Watson would know, but he couldn't imagine bothering her with anything as trivial as a chocolate design.

What was it Miss Watson had said about Linda? That she saw no boundaries.

Maybe that was it. Maybe he now saw a boundary that was behind him. One that had limited his vision. The problem was that every time he turned around, he saw Linda Hamlin's face.

It took him a moment to understand the he really *was* seeing her face.

"You came!"

LINDA COULD ONLY BLINK in surprise.

She hadn't actually come looking for Clive, but he seemed so happy about her arrival that she didn't want to gainsay him either.

Finally, in self-defense, she held aloft the map she'd been following. Rather than sending her and Thor to the fence line— the standard location for floppy-eared dogs to patrol—Captain Baxter had given her a map. Actually a book of maps—who knew the White House was such a vast complex.

"President Zachary Thomas and the First Lady are traveling— three days in Tennessee at her family's ranch," Baxter had rattled off his instructions so fast that only her military experience let her keep up with them. "Vice President Daniel Darlington is up on the Hill for the day. Go learn the White House. I want you and Thor familiar with every square inch." She was beginning to discover quite how tall an order that was.

Not wanting to bother anybody until she felt a little more sure of herself, she'd chosen to first explore everything below the Ground Floor. The West Wing was generally acknowledged to have three floors: the Ground Floor she'd entered on that included the USSS office and the Situation Room, the State Floor with the Oval and other key offices, and some more office space on the Second Floor. She'd discovered a labyrinth of two more stories below that, including several places where a Marine guard waited, so she decided to tackle those later. This included a massive new complex under the north lawn that had been built between 2010 and 2014 that she somehow doubted even her full-access pass would allow her into.

On second thought, rather than waving the book of maps aloft, with its bold "Secret" label on the cover, she tucked it in her vest pocket. She had no idea if Clive was authorized to even know that some of the areas existed.

"I'm so glad that you're here."

"You are?" She'd barely met him yesterday.

"I am," his big voice boomed about the tiny kitchen. "Welcome to my kingdom."

"Um, I don't want to appear rude, but isn't it a little small for a kingdom?" The room was perhaps twenty feet square, and that was only if it was stripped to the walls. Instead, every single nook and cranny was packed solid. White marble work surfaces, massive doors to walk-in refrigerators, and lots of fancy kitchen machinery. The center six-by-six-foot work table left barely enough room around it for two people to squeeze by each other.

On the few uncovered wall surfaces were pictures of too astonishing a variety to quite take in: peacock feathers, cobblestone streets in the rain, a postcard of modernist art. They all blurred together. Only the area around a portrait of a smiling man shaking Clive's hand seemed to rise out of the general noise.

"Nonsense!" Clive bounced to his feet. "It's a splendid kingdom! Come. I'll give you the grand tour, then I will ply you with tasty treats because you must come to my aid."

Linda tried to keep up, but three separate agendas in a single sentence seemed a bit much. "Maybe I should just..." She made the mistake of turning her head for a moment to wave down the hall that supposedly led to the Flower Shop. It was her next destination and then the three unlabeled rooms merely marked Storage beyond that. She'd found many interesting things that were marked that way on the map, none of them having to do with storing anything.

Her ill-timed distraction allowed Clive time to scoop up something from the counter and cross two of the four steps that defined the breadth of his kingdom to squat in front of Thor.

"He can't eat chocolate," she warned him off. "It's poisonous to dogs."

"I know that. How about a little bacon? I've been testing a savory treat, baked maple-glazed bacon with a chocolate drizzle that I haven't applied yet. Is this okay?" He held aloft the piece of bacon.

Thor was nearly shivering with anticipation.

"*Ja,*" she whispered to the dog, who practically snatched it from Clive's fingers the moment she gave him permission. Clive clearly knew to keep his fingers out of the way when dogs and bacon were involved. Technically, it was bad form to let anyone feed a Secret Service dog other than its handler, but Clive seemed okay.

Okay?

He was on his knees by her dog, thumping him lightly on the ribs as Thor made quick work of the treat.

"Now," in a deceptively smooth and light motion for a man of his size, Clive was on his feet once more looking down at her.

At six-four he seemed too large for the kitchen, and so close that she had to crane her neck slightly to look into his eyes. He was thinking hard about something, but she had no idea what. Then he had her arm in his grip and was tugging her over the threshold that only Thor had crossed.

In moments he was describing shining machines with words she'd never have applied to them or didn't recognize at all.

A grinder was neither for coffee beans nor smoothing down the side of an M-ATV where a bullet had pierced the heavy armor.

Conching was something done for days on end though she didn't understand what or why.

The tempering vat didn't seem angry at all.

"In the past, the White House Chocolate Shop has always relied on the production of chocolate by others. Chefs took the finished product in bulk and worked it from there. Whenever I can, I step back earlier in the process. I don't have room for a cocoa nib roaster, but I have control of the rest of the line after that point. Here, I'll show you the difference."

He pulled on a latex gloves before reaching into one of the coolers. On a tiny white plate, he placed three bite-size pieces of chocolate.

"Taste these. Start with that one," he pointed.

Unable to pull back from the rushing vortex that was Clive Andrews in his element, she gave in and tasted the first one.

"Nice enough, right? Melts well. Smooth on the tongue. A little crunch when you bite it. Swallow and the flavor lingers for several moments."

She tasted all of those things, none of which she'd ever noticed before.

"Now, a sip of plain seltzer to clear the palate," he handed her a glass that he'd been pouring. "This should be lime sorbet, but I don't have any handy at the moment."

When she opened her mouth to protest that she didn't have a palate, he popped a second piece in her mouth.

"Notice the sharper snap when you bite on it. There are hints of the terroir. A suggestion of vanilla, though I haven't added any to this batch. The melt is slower, teasing at your senses as it unfolds. When you finish, it lasts, convincing you... Almost whispering in your ear," he leaned in and did just that. "More. Eat a little more."

She tried to pull back, but her body said to lean in. The two canceled each other out, but she wouldn't soon forget the way his voice lowered and teased like the chocolate did.

"More seltzer now. And now the third piece."

She didn't even make a pretense of reaching for it, instead just opening her mouth and closing her eyes as he popped it into her mouth.

"Bite it," he whispered.

She did. The snap was fresh and crisp. Behind it came a tidal wave of sensations. So smooth, it was almost like cream. Flavors wandered by, teasing, enticing, promising...and delivering. She breathed in through her nose and the flavor built and unfolded. It was just chocolate and vanilla, but it seemed to unravel and entice with so much more. She didn't know what any of them were, but they were both magnificent and subtle in the same moment.

"Now notice—"

"Hush," she reached out and clamped her hand over his mouth. "I'm having a moment here."

His smile tickled against her palm.

CLIVE HAD LONG AGO LEARNED the power of good chocolate over women. But never in his life had he so enjoyed watching one eat it.

When Linda closed her eyes, her face softened. The fiercely focused Secret Service professional revealed an unexpected gentle side—transformed from brittle, sharp-edged sugar work to smooth chocolate sculpture. No longer bundled in her jacket against the January chill, her sleek athleticism still defined her, but it was no longer all of who she was.

Then she opened her eyes. Between one eyeblink and the next, Sergeant Hamlin returned. She pulled her hand away from his mouth as if she'd been electrocuted.

"Okay. That was tasty. I'll admit that."

He couldn't help laughing. She might think she was all the tough dog handler, but now he knew better. He'd seen the woman behind the wall. And he wanted to see more.

"I have work to do. Thanks for the chocolate." And that quickly, she almost slipped out of his reach.

"Wait!"

"For what?" Linda turned to look at him from halfway out the door. The woman moved as if attached to a teleporter.

"I have a problem."

"The third item on your agenda."

"I have an agenda?"

She rolled her eyes at him, but he still didn't know what she was talking about. Under normal circumstances his next agenda might be how to get Linda Hamlin out to dinner, then into his bed, but in her Secret Service mode that wasn't going to happen.

He thought about reaching for her, but that too had shifted.

One moment she'd had her hand over his mouth—a teasingly gentle touch. So close that he could smell her. Unscented soap and shampoo left her own natural flavors to fill the air around him: the softness of honey and the warmth of fresh ground chili powder mixed with the freshness of new-fallen snow. She presented the most evocative sensations he'd ever encountered.

The next moment she was...herself. Half out the door and all about getting on with whatever business had led her past his shop.

"You said you needed my help."

"I did?" He did? "I do."

And he'd think of why in a minute, but if that was enough to hold her in place...

"Oh. Right," he moved back to the stool at the counter in front of his notepad, hoping that would draw her back into the shop.

She waited at the threshold. Well, if that was the best he was going to get, it would have to do for now.

"I need to make a special dessert. Something...relevant."

Again, the waiting silence that he was learning was Linda's answer to so many questions.

"The leaders of Vietnam, the Philippines, and Japan will be here next week. Something about some islands. Do you know why?"

"Why would I know that? This is my first day in the White House."

"Do you know what islands they'd care about?"

"For those three together? Probably the Spratlys. China has claimed them though they lie six hundred miles south of the People's Republic. They've dredged the reefs to build islands, one of which is now a heavily equipped military base offering them a significant forward projection of air and naval power. They've done all this despite United Nations' rulings that they didn't have the right to do so."

Clive could only blink in surprise. "Why would they do all that?"

"It extends their territorial control. For one thing, it places them at the center of a major oil tanker route reaching all of the way back to the Persian Gulf. They want to protect that supply chain as well as they can in future years. Possibly even preempting all three of those countries' supplies for their own benefit. Taiwan's and Korea's as well, for that matter. Without massive oil imports, there *is* no China, no matter how fast they burn coal."

She'd already completely shifted his understanding of the upcoming meal. A white chocolate egg with a bourbon mousse was completely irrelevant to the proceedings. New Birth had nothing whatsoever to do with this kind of problem. He needed to completely rethink it.

He could feel her watching him, but he didn't know what to say. How many of his desserts had he delivered with such little understanding of what was actually occurring upstairs in the State Dining Room?

Between one eyeblink and the next, his doorway was emptied.

Linda and Thor were gone as if they'd never been. He rushed to the door and caught only the briefest view of the two of them moving silently down the hallway before they turned a corner and were gone. So he hadn't imagined everything—she actually had been here.

He returned to his marble counter and looked down at his blank sketch pad trying to visualize what *did* belong there.

Except it wasn't blank.

His earlier doodle was of a small dog and just a hint of a woman's face no clearer than a ghost's.

"WOULD YOUR DOG LIKE A BISCUIT, my dear?"

Linda checked her map again. White House Residence, Subbasement Two, Room 043-Mechanical.

Then she looked back at the woman. She was tall, silver-haired, and had a pleasant smile. She waved a hand at a ceramic cookie jar in the shape of Snoopy's red doghouse, complete with the dog himself lying on the ridgeline as a handle. It sat on a small walnut side table.

Room 043-Mechanical had a ceiling of tangled pipes mostly lost in overhead shadows. But the room itself was warmly lit by a gas fireplace set inside a white-and-gray marble mantel at the far end. An old, disused looking desk sat close by the door, with a lone stool in front of it. Beyond that, a long room led past several bookcases to a cozy sitting area. Deep, cheerfully floral armchairs sported lace doilies over the arms.

Linda hesitated and inspected the shadows more carefully. Weapons of war were collected along the tops of some of the bookcases closer by the desk. Not just war, but clandestine war. They were the weapons that might have been used by an assassin or a spy. The Arsenal knife, with a .22 six-shot revolver built into the handgrip. A Ruta Locura single shot .22 LR rifle that could break down into a pair of carbon-fiber tubes—stock and barrel— no bigger around than her thumb and each as long as her forearm. Add a scope and it still weighed under a pound and a half. Utterly lethal and very hard to detect. It made the sniper rifle from *The Day of the Jackal* movie look clumsy.

Deeper into the room, the Tiffany lamps with their cheerfully colored shades lit framed portraits of women. Some in evening gowns, others in military uniforms.

"Yes, I'm sure Thor would enjoy a treat," Linda agreed to buy herself a moment longer to inspect the curious collection and the woman in the midst of it.

The woman made a show of lifting the lid and selecting just the right dog biscuit, then handing it off to Thor. He took it delicately from her fingers, rather than the sharp snap of Clive's bacon, before lying down to happily grind it into the room-filling, white Persian rug.

"Would his handler like some tea?"

She could only nod. Linda's head was spinning. She'd abandoned her basements-first plan after escaping Clive's chocolate shop. That had sent her tramping all through the upper floors of the Residence, feeling like a voyeuristic intruder.

Still uncomfortable approaching Clive's shop, she and Thor had investigated the East Wing from the top story First Lady's offices down to FDR's bomb shelter below the northeast lawn. A small plaque had informed her that it was rated to withstand a five-hundred-pound bomb—early WWII had been a kinder, gentler era in some strange ways.

Deep in the lowest basement of the East Wing, she'd turned away from the tunnel leading to the Treasury Building and instead followed the one that ran from the FDR shelter below the East Wing into the lowest level of the Residence, and beyond that, connected to the West Wing.

Deep under the lawn between the East Wing and the Residence, she passed The Truman Shelter. It had been built with nuclear weapons in mind and was significantly more substantial, if little more welcoming than FDR's concrete cube. It was set up as a complete safe room, but it too stood with its door open and no guard in attendance. Another part of the White House's buried history that none of the public would ever see.

Once more beneath the Residence itself, she and Thor had investigated air conditioning and heating machine spaces. She'd fed him a snack from her bag and let him rest for a while outside the elevator machine space.

She'd carefully avoided Clive's shop, though she could still feel his smile against her palm. It seemed to belong there. She wanted to go back. Taste another piece of his magnificent chocolate and perhaps see if his smile tasted as good as it felt.

Whoa! Where had *that* idea come from?

She hadn't been in a relationship since RAF Lieutenant James. Her team had been stationed with the British attack helo pilots at Kabul for six months, and she'd spent three of them happily in his arms whenever they were both on base. He'd been like the first of Clive's chocolates: not deep, but definitely nice enough while it lasted. There had never been a second-chocolate-level relationship for her. Something inside her was broken that didn't allow for any of those. Her emotions were broken, just like her mother's—a sour taste indeed.

Once more on the move, she'd rounded a corner past Electrical Switching Control in the lowest subbasement of the Residence and—stepped into a Victorian tea room complete with a silver-haired matron dispensing dog treats.

"Please, Miss Hamlin. You have walked a long way. Take a seat."

"You know who I am." A pointless statement. Somehow the woman also knew she'd walked miles today exploring the President's House. Probably knew Linda's tour was barely half done even though the day was almost over.

"I'm Miss Watson," she didn't bother wasting breath to confirm her knowledge of Linda's name. She poured tea from a white porcelain teapot covered in sweet pea flowers. On a small table between the two chairs, she placed a matching plate with unadorned shortbread biscuits.

Linda could feel Clive's pained expression two stories above. He'd have dipped, sprayed, or sprinkled them with something. Certainly he'd add elegant little designs on the tops like the ones she'd spotted on the chocolates in a small cabinet he'd shown her.

"You have an...interesting office, Miss Watson." A Victorian sitting room in the lowest subbasement of the White House made that an understatement. A pair of hinged bookcases had been swung back against the walls of the elegant room. Linda saw that if they were closed, the sitting room would disappear and only the dingy but dangerous little office would remain.

"Thank you, my dear." Miss Watson sat in a chair across from her and picked up her knitting.

Linda focused on the picture above the woman's head. It was of a dark-haired beauty in a golden, quasi-Egyptian metal bikini.

"Is that…"

"Mata Hari. Margaretha Geertruida MacLeod. Falsely accused, tried, and executed by the French for being a double agent—15 October 1917." Miss Watson didn't look down at her knitting, instead watched Linda intently. "They needed a sacrifice to their flagging morale, so they shot Mata Hari for being a former wanton during a time of constricting morals as much as anything else."

Inspecting other photos that hung about the room, Linda decided that some questions were best not asked aloud. But Miss Watson began answering them anyway.

"Marthe Cnockaert, WWI—specialist in explosives." Miss Watson indicated another image with a flick of the end of her knitting needles. "Sarah Emma Edmonds was an American Civil War master of disguise: male, female, black, white. Manuela Sáenz, 1800s—a fascinating and dangerous woman who destroyed a leader in Peru and was instrumental in creating Simón Bolivar in Venezuela. Nancy Wake, WWII. One of the most highly decorated servicewomen of the war, she topped the Gestapo's most wanted lists."

Who was Miss Watson that she had a room decorated with portraits of female spies?

Linda decided that her best option was to keep quiet and sip her tea. Thor, done with his biscuit, looked at her longingly until she gathered him into her lap. He sighed happily and flopped backward with his head in the crook of one of her arms and appeared to fall instantly asleep. He acted as if they'd been together a lifetime rather than twenty-four hours.

The clicking of the knitting needles stopped abruptly and Linda became aware of Miss Watson inspecting her closely.

"What drives you, Miss Hamlin?"

"I'm not sure what you mean. Dogs, I suppose."

"That answer is too easy, Miss Hamlin. Do you not find it so?"

"I can't say that I ever thought much about it."

"Oh, that's unlikely."

Linda blinked.

"Come, my dear. You are sitting in a library built upon histories of the exploits of the world's greatest spies, male or female. Some worked for intelligence gathering, others in undercover roles to take down hated regimes. Some of them hated *our* nation, yet they too adorn these walls. Runway model Anna Chapman—2001-2010 in London and New York for the Russians," she indicated a striking redhead posed in black leather pants and a lacy bustier while holding a chromed MP-443 Grach pistol as if she knew how to wield it. "Ethel Rosenberg and Ruth Greenglass—Manhattan Project for the Soviet Union. Wild Rose Greenhow—a noted spymaster for the Confederacy versus Elizabeth Van Lew who served a similar role for the Union. A woman of such caliber as yourself has most assuredly thought long and deeply."

Miss Watson finally pointed a knitting needle at the center of Linda's own chest like an attack.

"I'm not a spy."

"If you were, you wouldn't be here—though your picture might be. But your illustrious career leaves little reason to suspect your loyalties. My question is rather what *are* you, my dear?" The pointing needle turned once more to the mundane task of turning linear yarn into a three dimensional object.

The contrast of the inquiry couched as a mild threat made Linda inspect her tea. Her cup was only half empty, but she tested herself to see if she felt woozy or drugged. The room didn't spin.

She felt no more inclined to speak than normal. She closed her eyes and felt no different. She—

Miss Watson snickered quietly.

Linda opened her eyes.

The needles had again stopped clicking and Miss Watson was using an embroidered kerchief to dab at the corners of her eyes.

"What?"

"Watching your imagination is lovely, my dear," she barely managed over her quiet laughter.

"My—" Miss Watson had observed her thoughts. If not a mind reader, then she was certainly well trained in observing human expression. As well trained perhaps as Linda herself was at reading the signals of a dog's feelings. And that kind of training implied...

She scanned around the room once, twisting to make sure she didn't miss any of the pictures tucked on shelves or hanging over the mantelpiece.

"Where is your photo?"

Miss Watson's laugh brightened even more, leaving her unable to speak at all.

"Oh, that will teach an old woman," she fanned herself with her handkerchief once she had mostly recovered her composure. "After all these years, you would think that I knew better than to make assumptions. You are the first to ever unmask me." Then she unclipped a gold locket from about her neck, flicked open the cover, and gazed at it a moment before handing it across.

Linda looked down at the two tiny images within. One was of a young and beautiful woman. Though it was black-and-white, it was easy to imagine her brilliant blue eyes looking straight out of the picture from the cargo bay of a Vietnam era UH-1 Huey helo. The other was a closeup. In that one, she looked severely Russian: her blonde hair pulled sleekly back, sitting in the lap of a terribly handsome Soviet-era general with two stars on his golden shoulder boards.

"The first was shortly after my return from my third undercover mission to confirm the number of prisoners at the Hanoi Hilton and other camps, gathering intelligence used during negotiations at the Paris Peace Talks. Sergei, on the other hand," she sighed softly and a smile lit her features. "Poor Sergei had no secrets from me. Not once did he suspect any of my secrets."

Linda closed the locket and handed it back.

"You are more than you appear to be, Miss Watson."

"The best of us always are, my dear. We always are," she placed the locket once more around her neck and returned to her knitting.

CHAPTER FOUR

$\mathcal{I}$t took Linda two full days to complete her White House tour and another to walk the outer grounds. Jim, Malcolm's handler, had been right. Every single moment was humbling.

Each night—while Thor snoozed on her feet in their temporary billet near the James J. Rowley Training Center—she had studied the book of maps until it was embedded clearly in her mind alongside other locations she'd had to scout over the years. It was an uncomfortable feeling to have the White House overlaid in her mind with sections of Kabul and Lashkar Gah, Afghanistan, as well as Mosul, Iraq, where the Rangers had served as "advisors" during the bloody battles clearing out ISIL.

She'd learned a lot these last few days. The Emergency Response Team dogs worked from vans parked around the perimeter of the fence line and from strategic emplacements inside the fence, allowing them to spring into action at a moment's notice. The floppy-eared sniffer dogs were afforded no such luxuries.

After the half-hour ride in on the Metro, they stopped off first at the USSS offices six blocks from the White House. There they transformed from a woman and her dog into a fully kitted out Secret Service team. Leash was traded for USSS harness that proudly announced Police K-9 on the Kevlar vest that wrapped down over the dog's vital organs (though it had taken them some time to find one small enough for Thor). For herself it included a six-pound Dragon Skin vest—the best armor in the business no matter what the Army politicians said about the twenty-two-pound "lightweight" IOTV or the thirty-plus-pound full version. Adding basic weapons to that, she was ready for duty—a day on the fences.

It was what she was coming to learn was a typical DC day in January: low thirties rising too slowly to low forties, clear blue skies with a high hint of cirrus clouds heralding incoming weather from the Atlantic.

Thor tugged ahead as they were walking to the fence line.

"Going to be on our feet all day, there's no need to hurry."

But he wasn't listening. Not at all. Instead...

Normally, he wandered about just like any other dog, checking out lampposts and fire hydrants for messages on the dog-pee telegram network. Only when she told him *seek* did he forget about that and go hunting explosive smells.

But what if he'd found one of those smells on his own?

He still moved ahead in the slight zigzag that so disconcerted oncoming pedestrians intent on their to-go coffee and reaching work on time. But she knew he was weaving to make sure that he wasn't straying from the strongest centerline of whatever scent he'd found.

Linda risked a quick glance around but spotted no other Secret Service agents on the move. This was really happening and she had no backup. What if she caught up with Thor's quarry before they reached the fence line? She rested a hand on her Taser, but using a device that delivered several thousand volts into someone wired up with explosives wasn't her first choice. The secret to dealing with a bomber was to tackle the individual, controlling both of their hands from the first instant, in case they were clutching a dead man switch or reaching for a trigger.

She felt a decade of combat training slip over her like a favorite jacket. The blast of adrenaline made her hyperaware of her surroundings. She began assessing and recording every possible relevant detail from crisscrossing pedestrians to the models of cars moving along the road. Her mind cleared of everything except the moment: possible attackers, assets, terrain, safe hides, minimum threat to innocents.

Thor picked up the pace, weaving less and less as he homed in on his quarry.

He knew nothing of the dangers involved. His sole mission was to locate the explosives and then receive a doggie treat for his vigilance.

Linda eased him back.

Thor proved just how strong his legs were in his drive to move ahead, but she kept him at bay.

They crossed 15th Avenue just north of the Treasury Building. No rental vehicles pulled to the curb where they shouldn't be. Everyone's car windows rolled up against the cold morning rather than lowered to allow firing a weapon. Once across the traffic, Thor followed the scent into the pedestrian-only area of Pennsylvania Avenue between the White House and Lafayette Square.

As pedestrians peeled off with each turning, her field of possible targets narrowed.

She was down to eleven. Two blondes with cell phones out and chatting together while barely watching where they were going (unlikely). Three couples, one holding hands and two holding coffee cups (unlikely). Three solos: black wool coat to his knees, gray suit, and brunette with a stylish jacket.

CLIVE EMERGED from the underground entrance at the Metro Center station. Though he'd ducked underground less than twenty minutes ago in Friendship Heights at the northwest corner of DC, it was always a surprise. Today, he'd descended in darkness and emerged in the light. Sunrise happened so much faster in the winter here, especially when compared to San Francisco.

Though it felt as cold as a San Francisco fog.

A pleased shiver rippled over him. It made him experience a touch of homesickness even if there was no longer any reason to return. But even that sad reminder enriched the flavor of the breaking dawn.

He disgorged onto the street with the other Washingtonians, bursting forth from the escalator like a hundred fronds of a chocolate lacework, dispersing into ever-tapering clumps but joined by others until their overlapping paths created an invisible lacework upon which the city was laid.

Interconnections.

He still hadn't resolved his dessert for the State Dinner, but he liked the word "interconnections."

He had consulted with Chef Klaus about it. As Clive had feared, no neat answers to the dessert had been forthcoming, but for his troubles, a chocolate course had been added to the front of the menu. That alone had required most of a day. He'd started with an old Jacques Torres recipe that his mentor had cooked for Julia Child's show as a young man: caramelized bananas in a milk chocolate soup with a baked meringue topping. It was good, reliable, but it was a dessert soup and Klaus wanted something for the first course. He didn't have much luck adapting it, so he finally abandoned the idea and went looking elsewhere for a first-course chocolate solution.

As the White House's head chef, Klaus was insisting on a European menu, which made the various Mexican chocolate *mole* soups unwelcome candidates. After a long afternoon of experimentation, Clive had finally recalled a white chocolate-pomegranate *baba ghanoush* that he hadn't made since school. A little testing, and now with a much more experienced palate, he had created a very pleasing dip by the end of the day. It was Middle European rather than strictly European but, with the substitution of individual miniature French baguettes rather than pita for the base, Chef Klaus had agreed that it was acceptable— high praise for him.

Another day since he'd met Linda had been filled with processing chocolate. The concher had finished a batch of Forastero nibs and had needed a thorough cleaning before he could start on the rare shipment of Criollo that had come in from Venezuela. That country was in such disarray that he rarely got his hands on any and he missed the flexibility that the rich flavor provided.

Then, he'd made a batch of chocolate-dipped lemon-coconut macaroons. The First Family was always partial to their sweets after returning from a trip and he tried to keep them pleasantly surprised.

He wasn't sure quite what had happened to the last day since meeting Linda with Thor. Perhaps daydreaming about the brunette whose dog had led her into his shop for such a brief instant. And the incredible way she had softened as he fed her chocolate. Softened...then hardened faster than an overchilled ganache. Gone so quickly that she almost hadn't been there.

It was ridiculous. He'd met her twice for less than ten minutes each time, but she left a greater impression than a Jacques Torres praline. It seemed that everywhere he looked he saw her, or at least impressions of her.

Even now, as he streamed toward the White House in the company of hundreds of others, he could spot a flounce of brunette hair just her color and in the same carelessly unfettered cut.

He hurried across 14th pushing the limits of the Don't Walk

countdown. Normally he was glad to wait and simply enjoy the day, but not today.

The glimmer of shining fifty-percent-cocoa brunette was still moving quickly down the block ahead of him. It moved with a speed and determination that had his pulse and his hopes picking up a beat. It was very hard to run into a dog handler by chance while working in the White House kitchen. Even on the busy streets of a large city it was more likely.

Maybe, just maybe.

He'd long since learned to keep his stride short or he outpaced anyone with him. But to keep up with Linda—if it was her—he opened up his stride. He could cover ground quickly when needed, yet still he only gained on her slowly.

A chance gap down the half block of crowded sidewalk gave him a full view of the woman for just an instant.

It *was* her.

No one else that he'd ever met had that head-down determined walk so completely integrated into their stride. Was he shallow that he also knew her fabulous figure from behind could belong to no one else? Perhaps, but it was true. Three days ago, when she'd disappeared from his chocolate kitchen doorway and he'd hurried out into the hall to see her striding away, she had stamped an indelible impression on his memory. As fine a vision as when she'd been walking toward him. She made him smile, delectable from every angle.

She slowed abruptly, causing a snarl in the normally smooth flow that was commuter foot traffic, causing her to briefly disappear from view. When she reemerged, their separation had halved. Then he missed the crossing at the corner of 15th and the White House Gift Shop and was left at the corner while President Zachary Thomas' face stared at him from a dozen plates in the display window.

As if he needed a reminder that he was focusing on a woman rather than his job.

"Morning, Thor. Hey there, Linda. Long time no see." Malcolm and Jim from the first day's fence line. He came off the corner of Pennsylvania just as she crossed it and left the fence line to come greet her.

Relief washed through her. She was about to open her mouth to explain what was happening when Malcolm veered sharply sideways, almost jerking the leash from Jim's hand.

Jim grunted once in surprise, then his gaze shifted from his dog to Thor and then to her face. No question, just a blink of surprise. Malcolm had found a scent and the handler had understood the cue.

With quick slices of her hand, she indicated the backs of her three "most likelies."

He tried veering Malcom off to the side, but the springer spaniel wasn't having anything to do with it. All the confirmation either of them needed.

Blondes peeled off toward the White House, as did the couple with the coffee cups. One of the other couples stopped to take a picture in front of the statue of Lafayette—the French hero of the American Revolution.

That left one couple and three solos. One of the solos peeled off, the brunette, but neither dog followed.

The other two—Black Wool Coat and Gray Suit—continued as if in flight formation, continuing along Pennsylvania Avenue toward Blair House, where foreign dignitaries were frequently housed. She vaguely remembered yesterday's briefing that the Japanese Defense Minister was already in residence to help prepare the way for the upcoming State Dinner. Or perhaps arriving early to make sure that the Japanese PM could lay claim to the Blair House accommodation so close to the White House rather than being placed in the Hay Adams across Lafayette Square.

Then the two targets veered more deeply into the park.

She glanced at Jim, who offered her a small shrug as if to say, "Your find, your call."

If *only* Thor had alerted to the scent, she might have hesitated. But with both dogs catching it…

That's when she had an idea.

She pulled Thor back, much to the dog's dismay, then slipped the release on his harness. The moment before he took off, she whispered *"Fassen! Ruhig!" Attack! Silent!*

The small dog raced after the target, and in a dozen very small bounds, lunged at the back of Mr. Black Wool Coat. He grabbed a mouthful, then dug in all fours and yanked.

Because Thor hadn't made a sound, the man almost fell over backward in surprise.

His briefcase fell to the ground as he tried to turn and see what was going on.

Japanese. Five-seven. Black hair to just above the ears. Particularly prominent cheekbones. Squinting against the bright sun—now in his face—his left eye closed first. His hands were small and exposed, no gloves despite the cold weather. Perhaps to make sure he held tightly onto the briefcase—even though he hadn't.

Linda jammed Thor's harness into the front of Jim's partially open jacket—didn't he get that it was freezing out?—then trotted up, "Secret Service Police. Are you okay, sir? I've got him," She snatched up Thor before the man could kick him. She let him wrestle with the man's coattails for a moment longer before whispering, *"Gute Hund,"* just loudly enough to get Thor to settle and release. It should look as if she was the good cop, saving a passerby from a stray dog.

Meanwhile, Jim's Malcolm had stepped up to the man's briefcase and promptly sat. *Bad cop.*

Jim moved up to block the man reaching for it.

"I have diplomatic immunity. You can't touch that," Black Wool

Coat protested. Gray Suit had continued on his way with hardly a sideways glance.

"May I see your card, sir?" Jim put all of his six-plus feet and workout body to good use, looming over the small Japanese man.

While he was fishing in his pocket, she set Thor down. "Get along, you," she said in English, then followed it softly with "*Such,*" in German. Thor sought. It took him three steps and he sat down in front of the briefcase beside Malcolm. Double confirmation on the explosives.

"Isn't that sweet? They're friends," she did her best to make it a coo, which sounded utterly ridiculous. Probably meant she'd gotten it right.

The Japanese man turned to look at her. Jim took the opportunity to call the bomb squad. As they were on twenty-four-hour alert and were stationed less than six blocks away, they'd be arriving very quickly.

Again the man reached for his briefcase.

Rather than telling Black Wool Coat not to touch the case, Jim called out, "*Pass auf!*" Malcolm twisted to face the man and let out a snarl befitting a much larger dog.

Thor also reacted to the command and added his higher voice to Malcolm's.

She stepped firmly between the man and the dogs.

"We seem to have a problem here, sir. Would you mind explaining it to me?"

Already she could hear the bomb squad's sirens roaring toward them along New York Avenue.

CLIVE WASN'T REALLY PAYING attention to what was going on at the other side of the morning crowd, he was just glad that he was catching up to Linda. He hurried along the path to where she'd stopped close by Andrew Jackson's statue at the center of the park. The massive edifice was topped by a bronze of the two-term President and general of the Battle of New Orleans on horseback.

At his feet, close by the wrought iron fence protecting a circular lawn, Linda and Thor stood close beside another handler-dog team, chatting with a man in a long wool coat who appeared upset.

Thor glanced in Clive's direction.

Half a heartbeat later he was staring at the yellow end of a space age gun that Linda had pointed at his chest from less than ten feet away.

"Uh…"

"Damn it, Clive! Get out of here! It's not safe." She swung the weapon down toward the ground and he recognized it as a taser. He'd seen other Secret Service agents carrying them, but never thought about it much. Now that he'd stared down the barrel of one, then into the wielder's coldest dark eyes he'd ever seen, he'd be thinking about it in his nightmares for a long time to come.

"Why isn't it safe?"

As if in answer, two vehicles jumped the curb and raced across the square in their direction. The black suburban was unmarked, but there was no mistaking the equally black truck close behind it. "FBI Bomb Technicians" was emblazoned down the side in large gold letters and it towed one of those disposal trailers that looked like a six-foot steel sphere.

Capitol Police streamed in close behind them.

Some of the early morning crowd scattered in alarm, others moved forward to gawk.

And they were all focused in their little group's direction.

"Any other questions? Now get out of here." Linda holstered her taser and turned back to the third man.

Clive hadn't noticed him before—an Asian in a long wool coat. His face looked arrogant as he held out some form of ID. Clive had seen enough of them at the White House to recognize a Diplomatic Immunity card.

When the police came up to move Clive back, he went, but he didn't leave. He joined the gawkers at the safety perimeter and didn't care if the policeman rolled his eyes at him before walking away.

Already the bomb techs were pulling on those heavily padded suits they wore making them three times their normal size.

And still Linda stood close by the fallen briefcase that commanded the dogs' attentions. She wore no bulky body armor. She looked so fragile, standing in the center of the danger.

A robot rolled out of the second truck. Bright silver with long arms holding multiple cameras aloft. A yard long and equally high —it drove forward on four rubber tires.

And still no one was moving aside.

Clive wanted to shout a warning but had no idea what it would be.

"Move it, ma'am," one of the bomb techs called out. "And get your dogs clear."

Linda kept watching the Japanese, chronicling additional facial features until she could draw him from memory, even though Jim was holding his ID and calling it in to doublecheck that it was valid.

Goro Yamashita had stopped trying to retrieve his briefcase, but he also wasn't walking away. His hands, except for retrieving his immunity card, had reached into no pockets for a hidden trigger.

There was also something odd about his attitude. Arrogant and self-righteous, yes. But not fanatical in the way she'd come to recognize as "normal" among the true jihadists of Southwest Asia. He didn't strike her as a man who would blow himself up, yet he wasn't walking away to move outside any blast zone either. Linda judged that the hazard was low.

She called Thor to heel beside her and stepped straight into the man's personal space.

Yamashita gave way, backing up. Not even a single glance at the briefcase. It made it unlikely that there was some sort of a proximity detonator on his person that would trigger the explosives if he was too far away.

He dug in his heels at ten meters. "You are not authorized to touch that case."

Jim had him covered with a sidearm that he hadn't reholstered, so she risked a glance. The robot had reached the case and extended a camera eye to inspect it closely.

"I'm sorry, sir," Linda made an effort to recover her good cop role. "But I saw no markings on your briefcase that would indicate it was a diplomatic pouch."

"That's precisely what it is!"

Now she understood some more of the elements of the Secret Service training. As a soldier, she'd have believed him. But now she knew that if it wasn't clearly labeled, it wasn't technically a diplomatic pouch—a single fact of thousands they had spent these last months pounding into her brain. Without a label, once he'd dropped it, it had become a briefcase and nothing more.

But if they opened it and discovered a pouch inside, they'd have to return it unopened no matter what the dogs said about it. They couldn't even X-ray the pouch without breaking the 1961 Vienna Convention on Diplomatic Relations.

Leaving Jim to cover the man, she trotted over to the bomb squad's truck. Two TV vans had pulled up close behind it. At least the no-fly zone over the White House was keeping the news helicopters away. She didn't like staring straight into one of the camera lenses, even if the Capitol Police were keeping them back. She turned her back on it.

Why did they even bother with television anymore anyway? She'd left for war before cell phones became the standard form of news gathering. Now there were fifty or a hundred people recording every single move she made. She could either worry about someone catching something she didn't do perfectly... Or they could all go to hell.

She opted for the second choice and erased them from her mind.

"Who's your commander?"

"Talking to him. What do we know?" He was leaning over the robot operator's shoulder and didn't bother to look up.

"Japanese male. The briefcase triggered both of our dogs."

"Please don't use the word trigger around explosives."

"Got it. Both dogs alerted. He has diplomatic immunity. We're verifying that it's genuine. He has the card."

"Diplomatic...Shit!" He looked up at her.

"He dropped the case and it has no outer markings. If you open the case and there's a diplomatic pouch inside, we're sunk. But if you X-ray it while it's still closed..."

His smile was quick. "Some light in the day. Thanks, sergeant. We're on it."

CLIVE DIDN'T like the way the man's eyes lingered on her as she and Thor trotted over to rejoin their teammates and the man in question. The fact that his own eyes had been lingering earlier was...well...

Okay, maybe he could empathize with the bomb squad officer. In the nation's capital—the city most likely to have women looking their best this side of Paris and Milan—Linda stood out as being impossibly real. Designer clothes traded in for police gear. An attitude that didn't care what others thought of her. And a lethal edge which, of all unlikely things, was attracting him a great deal. Past lovers were casual memories, two ships in the night and all that. Nothing about Linda Hamlin said that was any part of who she was.

What did she see when she looked at the world?

Danger everywhere and everything a threat until proven otherwise?

He tried to see Lafayette Square through her eyes.

The sun was well up now, the sunlight had cleared the buildings to the east enough to light the five statues at the four corners and the center of the square. The grass was green and the concrete walkways were immaculate after being cleaned by the nighttime crew. Some people stood on the park benches to get a view of the excitement over the heads of gawkers who showed no sense of self-preservation.

Of course, neither did he. Except he did. A little. Linda was out there and he couldn't leave until he knew that she'd be okay.

The robot was tipping the case upright and a man in a bomb suit was rolling out a cart. Probably the X-ray machine he'd been able to overhear Linda talking about.

Some people were looking at their watches, cursing, and pushing through the encircling crowd to hurry off to work. His time was more flexible, and even if it wasn't, at the moment he didn't care.

If Linda saw danger everywhere, she must be overwhelmed by the amount of information. How did she filter it down? He scanned the area again. Of the entire crowd, only a few people stood out. Several hecklers were shouting for an arrest. Someone else had a placard on a tall handle, protesting against police brutality. He was waving it about injudiciously enough to have cleared a space around himself of people who didn't want to be brutalized by it.

The perpetrator himself stood with his arms folded over his chest, waiting. He wasn't watching his briefcase or the bomb tech. He wasn't watching the two dogs sitting at alert by their handlers' feet. He also wasn't looking at Linda. Instead he wore a smug half smile and faced the other dog handler.

Clive scanned for anyone else who wasn't behaving as might

be expected. There were too many people. Cell phones aloft, hecklers still heckling, police keeping a secure perimeter, and the bomb squad ignoring everyone while they worked through their meticulous procedures.

A third of the way around the circle, an Asian man stood at the front of the crowd. No phone aloft, no emotion on his face. His hands were unnaturally straight at his sides. As if he was standing at attention, but not in any US military form that Clive had seen around the White House.

Clive kept an eye on him as he scanned the rest of the crowd, but he didn't pick out any other anomalies.

Because he'd ended up beside the bomb squad on their initial arrival, moving away from Linda only after the police cordon had been set up, he was inside the bubble—a feeling he recognized from working at the White House.

He took a deep breath, finding a conviction somewhere inside him that was stronger than chocolate. Then he simply strode into the circle as if he belonged. It must have worked because he only saw twenty or so cell phones turning to track him, but no officers shouted at him to stop.

"Hi, Thor," he squatted down to pet the dog now sitting beside Linda. Maybe if he didn't surprise the dog, he wouldn't face the wrong end of a taser again.

Thor popped to his feet and leaned into Clive's knees hard enough that he lost his balance and fell over backward on his butt.

Linda looked down at him in surprise. "What part of get as far away as possible don't you understand?"

Thor decided it was a prime chance to sit on his chest and breathe doggie breath down into his face. He knew that his palate would be ruined for tasting chocolate at least for the morning—everything would taste like panting dog.

"Apparently this part," he looked up at Linda just in time to receive a cold, wet dog nose in one eye. "Yow! Cut that out you," he wrapped his hands around Thor and lifted him aloft so that he could at least sit up.

"What are you doing out here?"

"I saw someone who didn't fit."

"What?" Linda squatted down and took Thor from him, dropping the dog back on all fours on the concrete. Thor instantly bounded up to place his forepaws on Clive's chest. He'd have gone down again if not for Linda's support.

"I was like you."

"I like you, too, but this is a damned weird time to be telling me."

"No, I— Wait! You do?"

Linda huffed out a breath, which at least smelled of cheap coffee and a sugar donut rather than doggie biscuit. It was an improvement over Thor's, but not by much. He was definitely going to have to fix that for her. This was a woman who deserved delicate pastry and good hot cocoa.

"That isn't what I meant. I mean that I was trying to be like you. And I saw a man in the crowd who doesn't fit."

Linda didn't even look around. Instead she closed her eyes for a moment. Then she cursed vilely and looked back at him.

"Gray suit coat? Standing roughly past my right shoulder?"

"That's the one." How did she do things like that?

"Thanks, Clive. I should have seen that. I want you to leave now."

He swallowed hard. Was that all the thanks he was going to get? If he'd seen something important, it should more than—

"Go back the way you came. Quietly pick up a uniform cop and get behind Mr. Gray Suit, outside the crowd. I'll give you a ninety-second head start before I flush him."

Clive briefly pictured a flushing toilet and tried to imagine what that had to do with anything. Then he focused on Linda. She might not be a plumber, but she was definitely a hunter—a hunter of men. She was going to flush her quarry, as in make it run.

She rose, grabbing his hand and proving her surprising strength as she tugged him to his feet.

For just an instant they were chest to chest so that he had to look almost straight down to see her.

"And yes, I do like you. Now get out of here," she pushed him away, raising her voice for the last.

Ninety seconds later—as he rushed to be in position with two uniformed officers—Linda and Thor circled along the front of the crowd. His height allowed him to follow the progress by momentary glimpses of her beautiful hair. She was almost upon the man in the gray suit before he noticed. He faded back into the crowd quickly—straight into the officers' arms.

Clive could get to enjoy this.

CHAPTER FIVE

"*G*ood work this morning."

If one more person told her that, Linda was going to...she didn't know what but she was definitely going to do it. If she ever had the energy to get out of this chair again.

She'd made the mistake of dropping into a chair in the Secret Service Ready Room on the West Wing's Ground Floor and now couldn't find the motivation to get back out of it. There were only six agents in the room at the moment, and all of them had said the same thing already, so she was safe for the moment.

She and Thor had spent the entire day, except for a far too short pee break for both her and the dog—in the room at the opposite end of the floor.

The Situation Room—a place she'd never thought she'd ever see, even with her captain's instruction to learn the entire building—had been both more and less than she'd expected. The President's Briefing Room was but one small part of the Situation Room complex. There were secure phone booths just waiting for Clark Kent to turn into Superman, and meeting rooms for smaller groups, right down to two people. The biggest room by far was given over to the operations staff who sat at a two-tiered curved desk—three in front and three behind—each station with multiple monitors. These six watch officers were the heartbeat of the Situation Room, completely visible but never shown in the movies.

She and Thor had spent the entire day in the Briefing Room, deconstructing every moment of a situation that had lasted less than thirty minutes. The main events had lasted less than ten.

There had been a round robin of individuals. Captain Baxter. Harvey Lieber, freshly returned with the First Family, of course. A tall, slender, and somewhat terrifying woman—the White House Chief of Staff Cornelia Day—had also stepped in several times.

Secretary of State Mallinson had been of frustratingly little help. Every idea by anyone earned a ten-minute lecture on the geopolitical implications of the shifting relations among various international trade organizations.

The second man, Gray Suit, also had a Japanese diplomatic pass, but he appeared to be far less pleased about being apprehended. He was a career diplomat, stationed in DC for nearly two decades.

The bomb squad had learned nothing from the X-ray except for the block of explosive inside the briefcase. Oddly, there was no apparent trigger mechanism. There were some other materials in there—which might have been papers or might have been the outline of a diplomatic pouch.

This had earned them a thirty-minute lesson from Mallinson on the implications of violating the 1961 Vienna Convention as well as a byline history of various known times that a diplomatic pouch had been misused for the smuggling of weapons or hundreds of millions in American currency—the global bribery currency of choice.

Unable to gain sufficient resolution, the bomb squad had the robot deliver it into the bomb containment chamber that the explosives team had brought with them. The weight of the briefcase was only four kilos and the chamber was rated to a ten-kilogram explosion, so they locked it in and drove away out of her life. They'd take it to Quantico and blow it up out on the demolitions range.

A Secret Service tail confirmed that neither of the diplomatically immune terrorists—for so they were—had subsequently met with the Japanese Prime Minister at Blair House. The minister had, predictably, denied any knowledge of the two men. Nor had they headed up Embassy Row to the Japanese Embassy. Both men had turned instead for Dulles airport where they boarded a flight...to Beijing.

That had really sent Secretary of State Mallinson off the deep end.

Were they working for China? Attempting to disrupt the upcoming meeting about China's incursions into the South China Sea?

Was it merely misdirection and the two agents would board a connecting flight to Japan? Or some other country?

While Mallinson railed, the CIA Director had contacted his Chinese counterpart. China had agreed to watch them closely to see what they did, but it was outside of US jurisdiction and no longer her problem.

Linda's best guess was that, whoever the two men worked for, their next action wouldn't vary. They would step off the plane in Beijing with different identities than they had boarded and would blend into the disembarking crowd. The US had been unable to get an agent on the plane as the flight was full.

That had brought up another puzzle. To board a full flight, they already had to have tickets. So their mission had only been delivery of the explosives. If it had been more, they would have missed their flight. It had all been pre-calculated with an impressive nicety of timing.

Linda rubbed her eyes. The only light of the entire day had been when Clive had been brought in to discuss his part of the action.

Mallinson had been called away to obstruct someone else's effort at having a coherent thought, so at least he was spared that.

Clive had been practically shaking with nerves as he'd looked about the Situation Room wide-eyed. Rather than going with the impulse to hold his hand to comfort him—especially because she had no idea where *that* came from, completely aside from it being wholly inappropriate—she'd scooped up Thor and dropped the dog in his lap.

For a moment she'd been afraid Clive would hurt Thor with how hard he hugged the dog to his broad chest, but Thor merely snuggled in and then settled on his lap while Clive was interviewed. She wasn't sure how she felt about the attachment between him and her dog. No, she wasn't in the least bit sure about that.

Thankfully, he'd left out any comments about his saying he liked Linda, changing the reason that he'd initially gone to her. "I was just being nice, wanting to check in that she was liking her new job. I hadn't seen her in three days."

Had it really been that long? She felt oddly guilty about that.

She did her best to suppress her envy that he'd been freed after only an hour. She'd spent eleven hours being grilled—or lectured.

"You look done in," a deep male voice addressed her.

"A military mission debrief is ten times easier. And thanks. Exactly what a woman always wants to hear." She rubbed her eyes one last time before forcing them open.

Clive.

"Decided to brave the West Wing a second time?" She asked him.

He shrugged. "Might not have if I knew I needed an agent escort just to see you here."

"I've got him, thanks," she waved off the agent who accompanied him into the part of the building that his pass wouldn't admit him. A funny contrast. As a senior chef, he had one of the highest clearances available—Presidential Proximity without an agent escort. However, as a chef, he had no clearance to the political areas of the White House's operations.

"What are you doing here, Clive?"

"Checking up on you."

"I'm fine." Nothing a dozen hours of sleep wouldn't fix. Except for having the lesson driven home that terrorists weren't only on foreign soil. Nothing was going to fix that.

"You are fine," his smile said that he was talking about more than her general well-being. "But you don't look it."

"Again with the sweet talk."

"Should I whisper in your ear about chocolate ganache or hot cocoa?"

She gave a dutiful chuckle. "Might work on me at this point, who knows."

Ignoring the fact that they weren't alone, he leaned toward her until she half thought he was going to kiss her. Another image she didn't seem to mind. Instead, he placed his mouth close beside her ear and whispered with that luscious voice of his, "Shining chocolate ganache. Steaming hot cocoa. Dark cherry truffle. Butterscotch praline."

LINDA'S LAUGH WAS BRIGHT—DOUBLY so because it was so unexpected. Clive hadn't even been sure she could laugh. It filled the room and drew the attention of the other agents.

That was the moment that Clive realized what he had just done, flirted with a Secret Service agent while she was surrounded by other Secret Service agents. The heat rushed to his face, but he couldn't do anything about it. His cheeks seemed to burn.

"I—" There was no excuse for embarrassing her in her new workplace. "I'll just go now." He resisted the urge to sprint from the room but did make a point of using his long legs to advantage.

Except he had no idea where he was in the rabbit warren that was the West Wing Ground Floor.

People were streaming up and down the corridors. Some pulling on coats in the hopes of escaping at the end of the day before some new crisis trapped them. Others hurried by—clearly still caught up in the frenetic business of the government. No matter what he did, he felt he was getting in deeper rather than finding his way out. His quiet, safe chocolate shop seemed to get farther away with each step.

He turned a corner and recognized the Navy Mess as much by scent as anything else. In another direction he spotted the two Marines guarding the Situation Room. He'd almost fainted in there today, would have if not for Linda's kindness. Not a chance he was going anywhere near that.

He swung the other way and plowed squarely in Linda, bowling her over. Thor stood directly behind her, taking her out at the knees, and she tumbled backward through a door and then was gone as it swung closed.

Thor looked up at him in surprise at being suddenly separated from his mistress.

Clive looked at the sign on the door and knew that his day had, impossibly, taken a turn for the worse. It read: Men's Lavatory.

CHAPTER SIX

*L*inda wasn't quite sure how it had happened.

Clive had refused to stop apologizing until she'd agreed that he could take her out to dinner. It was one of the trigger phrases she'd learned long ago. In a guy's mind, "dinner out" meant "hopefully with meaningless sex for dessert." Her standard answer of "thanks but no way in hell" didn't appear with Clive.

Instead, she'd happily followed him to the kitchen beneath the Residence, which was apparently his idea of a dinner out.

It was late enough that the kitchen itself was quiet. A sour-faced man, introduced to her as Chef Klaus, offered her a scowl and Thor another before returning to his tiny office. An on-call chef puttered away in the pastry kitchen. The massive White House kitchen was theirs alone.

A stove with a dozen gas burners, two big grills, mixers almost as tall as she was with bowls that Thor could have slept inside. Multiple ovens with more controls than she'd ever seen before, an espresso machine that would be the envy of even a Starbucks barista, dozens of pots and pans hanging from overhead hooks, a

75

meat slicer, knife racks… It never seemed to end—everywhere she looked there was more kitchen equipment.

But there were none of the homey touches of Clive's chocolate shop. No pictures on the walls, no sketches taped onto refrigerator doors. It felt cold despite the warmth of the room. Without thinking about it much, she'd scooted her stool closer to where Clive was cooking.

Partly to watch him. His big fingers were surprisingly nimble as he selected, sliced, and seasoned. His hands looked as if they belonged to a stone mason or a US Ranger. But after years of hard use in the field, a Ranger's hands would be hard-pressed to do any fine work—except strip and clean a weapon, of course. Clive's massive hands appeared to fly as he sprinkled a pinch of salt into a heating pot of pasta water and then began building a sauce.

She also scooted closer because it felt warmer near him. Not just the burners roaring with bright blue flames. There was something about Clive that drew her in. His willingness to walk into an explosives danger zone to warn her of something he'd seen that she should have. What man did that? Clive Andrews. And what had he said when he arrived? That he was trying to be like her…intentionally! Why anyone would do that was beyond her, but Clive had. As to his saying that he liked her—in the middle of her first-ever diplomatic crisis—well, it was beyond strange.

While the fettuccini boiled, Clive thin-sliced and sautéed chicken. At the last moment he tossed in lemon juice, shallots, and slivers of lemon complete with the peel. Thor was just going to have to wait for dinner until they got home, but it was hard to care because it smelled so heavenly.

Then Clive pulled out some hamburger. "I'm not sure what to put in this, I'm not used to cooking for a dog."

"A lump of that, raw. That's grounds to win love forever. Uh, his love." If Clive noticed her stumble, he didn't comment on it.

Instead he laughed aloud.

"Ground beef as grounds for love. Good one."

Which she hadn't actually thought of as a pun.

"That is precisely what every man needs, the love of a good dog. Doesn't he?" Clive asked Thor as he set to work. He placed a fist-sized ball of burger in a small bowl—thankfully her fist and not his, which would be nearly the size of Thor's head—and quickly beat in an egg. Then he set it upon a white plate. Somehow, with those big hands of his, he quickly shaped it into an elegant form as if it was a tiny meat Bundt cake complete with spiral flutes up the sides and a hole in the middle.

Why was she feeling a fit of pique that he was doting on her dog and not on... She needed her head fixed.

"Does he like greens?"

"I...don't know. Most dogs do." She'd given him kibble and canned dog food so far. She'd only had him five days, nowhere near enough time to learn his preferences. Not even enough time to learn her own. The scramble of these last days had relegated her meals to pizza by the slice from the corner shop near her apartment. She'd often buy an extra couple slices to have cold leftovers for breakfast.

Clive held out a small piece of spinach. Thor roused himself enough in her lap to happily chomp it down. Clive diced up enough to fill the hole he'd shaped inside the raw hamburger patty. He crumbled bacon over the top, throwing more into the sauce for their own dinner.

"That looks good enough for me to eat, forget about the dog."

"For a good tartare, I would fresh chop a much finer grade of meat and add some more spice. I make a good one, I'll do that some other time." Clive just smiled as he scooped out the finished fettuccini, let it drain for a moment, then dumped it into the sauce pan.

As if he hadn't ever so casually dropped his plans that this wouldn't be a one-time event. His confidence was amazing, which she liked, but with none of the arrogance that typically went with it.

He stirred it a few times. Then, in quick, neat motions, he mounded the fettuccini in elegant twists on a pair of white plates. Finally he grated Parmesan cheese on the top.

"I thought you were a chocolatier."

"I am."

"But you can cook as well."

"Of course."

"There's no 'of course' about it."

"Why? What's the last meal you cooked?"

Linda puzzled at that. The last time she'd cooked, something fancier than frozen pizza or a can of soup…

Clive stopped halfway through mincing some parsley. "You do cook, don't you?"

"Well, the Army sort of took care of that for the last decade. Or Mom's maid the few times I was dumb enough to go home on leave."

"Please tell me that you are joking," Clive sounded deeply offended.

"I *can* cook…" Linda gave up. "Though, honestly, nothing fancier than scrambled eggs and burnt toast."

He squinted closely at her.

"What?"

"I've spent the last five days fantasizing about a woman who can't cook? That can't be right."

"It's true. You—" His words caught up with her. "You *what?*" Her shout was loud enough for Chef Klaus to stick his head out of his office, leaning out far enough to look around the big stand mixer between them and deliver a hard stare before turning back to whatever he'd been working on.

Clive didn't appear in the least abashed. "We're in the house that George Washington built. Even if he didn't live long enough to ever take up occupancy here, it's still his house, therefore I cannot tell a lie." He dressed the plates with little spears of asparagus that she hadn't even seen him preparing, and a thick slice of crusty bread.

"But—"

"Shall we take our plates somewhere more private?" Ignoring her feeble protests, he did one of those waiter things with a plate in either hand and Thor's plate resting on his forearm. Then he led the way out the back of the kitchen and along the Basement Hall toward his chocolate shop.

Out of options, she set Thor on his own feet and followed after him.

CLIVE DIDN'T KNOW how to slow down around Linda, but it seemed to be working, so maybe he shouldn't.

He'd gotten her out of the West Wing without getting down on his knees and begging, though he'd come close while fishing her out of the men's lavatory where her boss Captain Baxter had been washing his hands. The captain had merely raised his eyebrows as he looked down at his newest officer lying prone on the tile floor.

Clive really wanted to get her back into the Chocolate Shop, where he'd made a couple of special treats for her. He'd almost screwed that up with suggesting that they go out to dinner, because that's what a man did with an attractive woman in DC, right? Dinner, drinks, a goodnight kiss that might lead somewhere or might not. He knew from past experience that leading somewhere tended to happen with him.

He'd never really given it much thought. He liked women and women liked him. Easy-peasy. It never lasted…

He glanced over at Linda as she squatted to give Thor his plate of K-9 tartare. It was easy to imagine watching her doing that, feeding her dog, day after day. He'd never really thought about having the same woman around for the long term. He knew it was in his future somewhere, but the insane hours of being a world-class chocolatier were no less hectic than being a world-class chef. He'd never found a woman willing to put up with that for long, which was fine—he was always up-front about it so it was never a big issue. But with Linda in his kitchen, the future shifted somewhere much closer.

Maybe that was why he couldn't slow down around her. All of his smooth skills around women had turned into curdles and the clumsy bloom of over-refrigerated chocolate.

And now that he had her here, in his chocolate shop, his mouth had gone dry with a sudden lack of words.

"I think he likes it," Linda patted Thor as he started eating.

"What's not to like?" He watched her and couldn't think of a thing. He was being ridiculous, he knew, but his attraction to her pulled at him like a new confection recipe.

Then, rather than taking her seat, she stood and stared at him. "What's that look?"

"What look?" He rubbed his hand over his face and did his best to erase it.

"*That* look."

"So much for wiping it off my face. Eat," he pulled out a pair of stools from under the counter. After a moment's debate, he set them kitty-corner at his central steel worktable—placing them close but still facing each other.

"Evasion, Chef Andrews."

"Absolutely, Sergeant Hamlin."

"And you want me to let you off the hook?"

"Consider it payback for identifying that bad man for you."

She harrumphed but took her stool. "Okay, just this once." But her look said not a chance was this over. "You still owe me for dumping me into the men's room—not that I'm keeping score."

"Did you ever figure out what they were doing, or is that now some state secret you can't tell me about?" Clive went for the subject change.

"I wish it was. We don't know. And we're getting mixed signals on who they were working for. The Japanese have now disavowed both of their diplomatic passports based on today's actions."

"A little late for that, isn't it?"

"It is. Both men were gone long before it happened. Whether that is per a plan by the Japanese or an honest reaction to a betrayal is unclear. Mr. Black Wool Coat was new to the mission, but Mr. Gray Suit was a senior official who abandoned a long career the moment he stepped on that plane."

"Which explains why he was so angry when we caught him," Clive could still remember the moment. It was the only time he'd been involved in anything like that. He'd have been a basket case of nerves if it hadn't happened so fast—Linda spooking him, Mr. Gray Suit breaking through the crowd, the officers grabbing the man as Clive pointed him out, and finally his look of fury at being caught.

"Fury or dismay? It became the latter fast enough. We've seized his US assets, but those are unusually small for someone who has served in Washington for two decades, as if he knew he was at risk and had cleared out most of his holdings just in case."

"So, basically, no one is happy." Except him. The adventure had given him the narrowest sliver of insight into the richness of mysteries in Linda's world. Crisis, adrenaline, action, yet she'd remained perfectly calm and in control throughout. And having her in his shop was enough to make him happy for a long time.

"Well, Thor looks pretty happy," Linda pointed out. The dog lay on the floor licking his chops with a polished clean plate in front of him. "And me. This is fantastic."

He'd been wondering if she was eating it without even tasting. It wasn't anything much, but it had come together nicely from various kitchen leftovers. Klaus always kept a shelf of items that any chef working late could take advantage of for a quick meal. He was stretching it a little for an agent and her dog but, other than one of his patented scowls, Klaus had appeared fine with it.

"Clive?"

"Mm-hmm?" He had a mouthful of pasta at the moment.

"What you said earlier?"

"Mm-hmm?" *Uh-oh!*

"Why?"

He chewed and swallowed. No real question what she was asking, so he'd go for his honesty policy. "You're asking why I like you. Have you met many DC women?"

Her shrugs were expressive. This one reminded him that though she'd been out in Maryland for three months, her experience with DC was minimal.

"There's a sameness to them. The way I have always figured it, DC attracts two major types of women. Ambitious women deeply concerned with politics for one. The others are looking for a job that they could find anywhere else more easily but wouldn't have the prestige of being involved in the government—or the chance at a future president for a husband, because of course they can make the right man into that. Guess which type I normally meet?"

"The tall blondes."

"Well sure," he wasn't going to fall for that trap. "Who wouldn't? But I'm finding that now I've met a third type."

Linda did that narrow-eyed inspection thing of hers.

"Short brunettes who take obnoxious K-9 instructors and international terrorists all in the stride of a day's work without letting it flap them in the slightest."

"You like me because I don't fly off the handle around a man who is being an asshole?"

"It's a good hedge against the future on my part, don't you think?"

LINDA COULD ONLY BLINK. Every time she tried to corner Clive, to pigeonhole him somewhere in her mind, he didn't fit. He also didn't mind each time she caught him.

Tall blondes. It was easy to picture a tall blonde beside him. He was a tall, handsome man and would look exceptional with a beautiful woman on his arm. So why was he talking to her?

I like you.

What's not to like? he had asked of Thor's dinner—which had been sweet and thoughtful of him to make.

She turned the question around: what was there about Clive Andrews not to like?

The normal laundry list that washed men out of her life before they even got into it wasn't applying.

They weren't in the same unit.

Not even in the same branch of the service.

Her first two big issues no longer applied because she was a civilian now. They allowed fraternization within the Secret Service, provided it wasn't within a linear chain of command. But even that didn't apply to Clive.

There was a freedom to the thought that she hadn't experienced in over a decade. Every relationship in the military had a dozen ramifications: rank, reassignment, and the imminent threat of death that was definitely a factor to consider in Special Operations Forces. Yet, for the foreseeable future, she and Clive would both be stationed in DC. If things didn't work out, all she had to do was not come by his chocolate shop. The entire danger-scenario, risk-assessment part of her thoughts had been rendered meaningless by the simple act of leaving the military.

And without all of those obstacles in the way, she realized that she *did* like Clive as well. And she remembered a feeling, the memory of a smile that had continued to tickle her palm for the last few days.

"Clive?" This was a very low-risk environment. It was a freaking chocolate shop.

"Mm-hmm?" Now he was just messing with her, both of their plates were clear.

If she was going to do something, she should just do it.

She leaned forward and brushed her lips over his. He tasted of lemon and shallot. And his return kiss was warm and thoughtful, taking his time about it. He laid one of those big warm hands over hers where it rested on the cool steel table.

Clive was clearly a man who knew how to kiss a woman. She hoped that she returned even a little of the same as her bones slowly melted. With only the slightest tug on her hand, not even enough to shift it, he somehow had her body moving toward his.

The heat warmed her from the inside out and she shifted, being careful not to break the kiss. She wanted...

She *wanted.*

That alone was a miracle. A part of her she was sure was dead...*wanted!* She—who had never needed anything other than her dog and a mission—wasn't some kind of emotional zombie as she always thought. She actually groaned as Clive slid one of those wonderful hands onto her waist. If he tried to take her here and now, she wasn't going to stop him.

There was a sharp growl that she didn't think came from Clive.

Then a high "Eeep!" that she was fairly sure didn't come from her.

A growl from a dog.

Too high for Thor.

An eeep from—

She broke the taste of heaven and turned to see a young girl standing in the Chocolate Shop's doorway with her hand clamped over her mouth. At her feet, a Sheltie growled at Thor, who'd risen to his feet in surprise.

Linda snapped her fingers and signaled for Thor to sit and stay. He sat down, but strained forward to sniff at the new arrivals.

"Dilya," Clive sighed. His sigh seemed to include an entire conversation, but Linda had no way to interpret it. Her head was still trying to process the flash of heat awoken by Clive's kiss, and her higher-functioning, multitasking capabilities were not reporting for duty.

The girl wasn't as young as she first appeared—mid-teens perhaps. Very pretty. Dark skin and even darker hair that cascaded in long ruffles down to her elbows.

"Wow. He's well trained," she squatted down to Thor's level. "Okay to pet him?"

"Sure," Linda was surprised the girl thought to ask. Most didn't. "Thor, *Freund.*"

"Hi, Thor," the girl didn't even hesitate at the name, winning her several points. "Yes, I'm friendly. This is Zackie," she tugged on the Sheltie's leash, but Zackie was busy getting pets from Clive —apparently he wasn't lavishing attention on Thor just for her sake, but genuinely liked dogs. She'd been wondering.

"Zackie?" Linda asked.

"Sure. Named for the President by the First Lady back when they were still Vice President and girlfriend."

"President Zachary Thomas' dog was named Zackie by his girlfriend?"

The girl's amused giggle was answer enough. "Actually, Zackie is her dog. She only lets the President play with Zackie if he's been nice to her."

"And what does she call the President?"

"Why, Mr. President, of course." But Linda didn't quite trust the girl's blithe answer. She looked fifteen at most, yet the nuanced way she said it seemed unlikely for a girl of that age. She herself certainly hadn't understood the subtleties of grown-up relationships at that age—except that she wanted no part of anything like her parents'.

Then the girl looked up at her. She wore a hot pink sweater, black leggings, oversized boots, and a scarf knit in tiny rows of colorful splotches to match Clive's—a noisy combination that screamed youth. But her green eyes, caught by the kitchen lights, belonged to no young girl that Linda could imagine. She'd only seen such old eyes in…Syrian refugee camps. On kids who had seen things not even an adult should have to witness.

"I'm Linda," she held out a hand.

"Dilya," the girl offered in return, though it was clear she already knew Linda's name.

"You're the President's dog handler?"

"When they're traveling somewhere Zackie can't go. Or have too many meetings or stuff like that. They just got home from Tennessee, so I took her out to burn off some of her energy. She's fine on Air Force One, but riding in Marine One, even just the short hop from Andrews, always winds her up. Yes, I know," she turned to the dog and unabashedly used the high squeaky dog voice, "you just can't help yourself, can you?"

The little dog yipped happily and wiggled with delight at the attention. Under all that fur she was probably about the same size as Thor, but she seemed as young as her caretaker didn't.

"How did you get Thor to stay like that? He still hasn't moved. Can you teach me?"

"Um, sure. But Thor has had years of training."

"I've worked on Zackie ever since President and Genny Matthews left the White House and decided they no longer needed a nanny. I still get to babysit Adele whenever they're in town, once or twice a month. The First Lady and the former First Lady both work for the UNESCO World Heritage Centre, you know. So they always have all of these meetings. And President Matthews goes over to the West Wing and hangs out with the President or Vice President whenever his wife is busy. Which means I end up babysitting Zackie and a two-year-old. Terrible twos, they're really something, aren't they?"

"I wouldn't know," Linda was still puzzling at Dilya. It sounded as if she knew everything.

Clive had returned to his seat from playing with the dog.

"You've never played with babies?" Dilya looked at her in surprise. "Oh, right, you just got out of the Army. Who were you with?"

"A group called the 75th Rangers."

"Which battalion?"

"Third," Linda wondered again just who this teen was.

"Oh, I don't know any of those guys. I used to hang out with the 2nd Battalion Charlie Company when my mom was... Whoops! Sorry. We were never there. Never mind."

Linda looked over at Clive, who had the temerity to just smile at her.

"Her mom is Sergeant Kee Stevenson, formerly with the 160th Night Stalkers, now part of the FBI's Hostage Rescue Team." Then he glanced at Dilya, who was still playing with the dogs, and silently mouthed, "War orphan." Which explained a lot.

"Kee..." Linda's voice trailed off. Everyone in Special Operations knew that name—she was one of the top snipers anywhere. Which meant that her father, another former Night Stalker, was the Secretary of Defense. Okay. Dilya's knowledge and personality were making more sense in some ways, even if she was making less in others.

"You're the one who found the explosives this morning?" Dilya asked the dog.

"He was," Linda answered for him.

"Good doggie!" Dilya pet him some more.

Zackie had also apparently come to terms with the presence of another dog and closed the rest of the distance between them.

"*Spiel,*" Linda gave Thor permission to get up and play. With a single bound, the two dogs plowed Dilya over onto her back and proceeded to race loops around the small kitchen.

"Told you that Marine One wound her up," Dilya clambered to her feet and smoothed her scarf.

"That's just like Clive's," Linda couldn't help but admire it.

"She liked the one Mom made so much," Clive reached out and thoughtlessly flipped Dilya's hair into place, "that I knit one for her."

"You really can knit?"

"I CANNOT TELL A LIE," he raised a Boy Scout salute. At least not as long as she didn't ask him what he'd been thinking when he kissed her. During that he was thinking utterly ridiculous thoughts about a woman he barely knew. Things like there never being another woman for him. "Keep being nice to me, and I'll knit you a sweater someday."

"At this point I'd take a decent pair of gloves," she wiggled her fingers at him.

That would be safer. Knitting a sweater actually had a lot of potential baggage with it. He'd heard from a ton of knitters that when the knitter made a sweater for their boyfriend, the relationship had always seemed to end at the same time the massive effort of making a sweater did. Yes, mittens would be safer. He'd have to figure out Linda's hand size, maybe from the outline he could still feel from when she'd covered his mouth.

Linda Hamlin overwhelmed him in every possible way. Forthright in a city where everything was nuance and innuendo. Her emotions so clear that there was no questioning them. Okay, she couldn't cook, but the way she looked while eating his food was enough to motivate him to cook forever. And he hadn't forgotten how she looked while tasting his chocolate. And the taste of her... He was ruined for anyone else. It didn't matter that he barely knew her because he already knew so much about her.

"It's beautiful work," Linda was fingering Dilya's scarf once the dogs had settled down to clean themselves after the excitement— Clive couldn't agree more. Whatever creator had carved Linda out of DNA and the ether of the unknown had forged a stunning masterpiece.

Dilya was watching him strangely.

"You came for chocolate, didn't you, you scamp?"

"Caught," Dilya admitted freely. But her look said a great deal more that he couldn't interpret. He pulled a few pieces out of the small cabinet and set them on a plate on the marble counter. The chocolate bars had indeed gone away far more quickly now that he'd made them smaller, but Dilya had never shown much interest in them.

He was about to reach for a small to-go box, but Dilya sat down on a stool beside Linda. He wanted her to himself. He wanted to kiss her again and find out if the impossible was actually real. Clive was a worldly man who definitely knew better than to be swept off his feet. But "Linda with Thor" had done just that. In a few short days, his world had completely shifted.

Shifted?

It was like the first time he had tasted couverture chocolate. His world had suddenly made sense in an instant. Years of thinking that the world was comprised of just baking chocolate and eating chocolate. On his own, he'd improved until he could create flavors and textures that won amateur awards.

Then he'd tasted couverture. The exceptional quality and increased cocoa butter content provided astonishing results in sheen, snap, mellow flavor, and a creamy mouth feel. In that instant, recipes and techniques had reconfigured in his mind until he understood just what *was* possible. Chocolate had shifted from a world he understood to one that he couldn't wait to spend the rest of his life exploring.

Linda Hamlin was exactly like that. Until now he knew women and how to please them. They were fun, like an infinite variety of chocolate chip cookies. But he now understood just how much a woman could be—the perfect, ever-unfolding truffle.

He looked at her to see how she'd been transformed by his realization—but she hadn't.

Sergeant Linda Hamlin sat beside Dilya over peppermint truffles, talking about dog training techniques. They left the candies half finished when they clambered to their feet and stood side by side in front of their dogs. That certainly put him in his place.

"The finger snap does two things," Linda was explaining. "One, it lets the dog know that whatever you do or say next is for them."

"Same as calling their name first. Simple word association for dogs," Dilya nodded hard enough to make her hair swirl about her head.

"Right. The second thing it does is actually far more important —it gets them looking at you so that they can see the next command."

"Like in a Delta Force operation, when they wave a hand at the edge of someone's vision prior to giving a silent hand signal. Got it!"

And Clive knew that meant that she did have it. He'd been on the receiving end of her brilliance enough times to know that the teen missed nothing. Though how she'd ever been witness to a Delta Force team doing anything...

Linda took it right in stride. "Exactly. The next trick is that nothing can be ambiguous. You come up with a standardized set of commands and always use precisely those words: come, come here, come along you—they're always alerting on the word *come* so don't use any other."

"Or not. Zackie isn't so hot on come. Or stay. Or..." Dilya groaned at the dog's failures.

"Or not," Linda agreed. "And why don't they come when called, especially when you *know* that they know better? Because when we shift tone, they may think that it's a different word. And each time you use it differently, it dilutes the primary. A single, consistent *come* will outperform all of the others combined. When you do use tone, keep that same balance to the word and simply increase the emotional trigger of intensity for emphasis."

"Do I have to use German? I don't think the President speaks it. Though that could be fun, actually."

"Easy, girl," Clive warned. "He is the President and it is his wife's dog."

Dilya smiled in that way that he could never interpret. He knew that most women had a smile like that—one that men were welcome to think was agreement, no matter what they were actually thinking. That's when he remembered that the First Lady *did* speak German and might enjoy teasing her husband about his inability to command her dog. As usual, Dilya was three steps ahead of everyone around her. Except maybe Linda.

Clive sat on one of their abandoned stools and tasted one of the peppermint truffles. A good balance of sweet and bright mint. The mix of textures was good, the smooth crispness of the outer chocolate and the coarser but softer mint fudge center.

The contrast.

That's what was so stunning about Linda, that contrast between who she presented to most of the world and the brief glimpses she let him see.

He fished out his notepad as they worked with the dogs.

Zackie was having trouble focusing, but Thor's steadying influence and well-honed actions were already helping.

Contrast. Contrast and... What was it he'd thought of earlier? Interconnections.

Japan, Vietnam, and the Philippines on one side. China on the other. Tension, threatening to pull everything apart. Connection, pulling it back together. More than connection—interconnection. Where their differences made a new whole.

Linda and Thor—human and dog making an exceptional explosives detection team.

The West Pacific Rim nations unifying in some fashion that was new and different.

The Vietnamese Marou and Philippine Malagos chocolates together. Not blended. No. Use the white Marou and the seventy-two percent dark Malagos. Twist them around a Japanese Pocky-style biscuit to create a chocolate candy cane look, along with a unification of the three working together in a different way. Now that was getting interesting. He had no idea how to actually do it, but that was part of the fun.

He pulled out a larger pad from under the counter and began sketching out the likely techniques. He couldn't simply scale up the Pocky stick—the texture would be wrong. The delicacy of the biscuit was part of the Japanese finesse. And how to twist the two chocolates together without *melting* them together?

Clive was several pages in when he noticed the quiet.

The Chocolate Shop was dead silent. No, not quite, Thor's soft doggie snore sounded in the background.

Linda sat once more on her stool, her chin resting on her palm as she watched him. Dilya was nowhere to be seen.

"You're an interesting man, Clive Andrews."

"I'm hoping I'm more than that," he looked at a clock to see how much time had passed, but since he didn't know when they'd eaten or when he'd started drawing, there was no way to track how much time he'd lost. Chocolate did that to him.

"Come on," she said to him as she stood up. Nudging Thor awake so that she could retrieve her jacket that he'd been using as a doggie bed, Linda shrugged it on.

"Where are we going?"

"You're taking me home."

Clive could only nod.

CHAPTER SEVEN

*L*inda never made decisions like this, but as Clive unlocked his front door, she swore that she wasn't going to second-guess herself. Which, of course, meant that she couldn't stop doing it.

"Would it be inappropriate for me to ask why we're here?" Clive was standing in the center of his apartment's living room.

Thor began sniffing his way around the apartment as she also checked it out.

It was a very guy space. A leather lounger, built on the same scale as Clive—big—faced a large television. Football or cooking shows? She'd bet on the latter.

Beside his chair was a large collection of books in untidy stacks. She looked closer: dessert cookbooks. The walls were mostly decorated with—she moved closer—pictures of chefs shaking hands with Clive and of knit goods. A quick scan around and she spotted a tall, glass-fronted mahogany cabinet so full of yarn that it looked like a rainbow gone mad. A massive sweater of gray wool, covered in intricately overlapping cables, had been tossed on a couch.

"You really do knit."

"You're avoiding the question."

She turned for the kitchen. Inspecting that, even if she wouldn't be able to judge most of what would be in there, would be far more comfortable than answering why she was here. There was a splendid, lived-in quality to the apartment. Her own small studio could still pass military inspection.

"Linda," he snagged her elbow as she tried to pass by.

His simplest touch brought her to a halt. It was just them now. No chef peered at them from behind a mixer. No teen was likely to drop in, seeking chocolate and dog training tips. It was just them and she didn't know what to do about it. Her plans for some sex with an interesting man whom she liked felt foolish now that she was here.

It *had* been a while. Secret Service training had kept her hopping enough that she could brush off the various passes made by the other trainees. Those had also faded away as she'd worked through the course in half the normal time—many of them hadn't liked that. And before that in the 75th Rangers she'd...

Clive kissed her.

Her whirling thoughts slammed into focus. Clive. She'd been working with Dilya and giving her the basics techniques for training Zackie when Dilya had done a teen thing that Linda remembered all too well from her own past. The girl had suddenly realized that she was learning something from an adult and that didn't fit with a teen's independent self-image. Between one eyeblink and the next, Linda had been alone with Clive, who was so immersed in his drawings and notes that someone could have indeed bombed the White House and he probably wouldn't have noticed.

Clive. His kiss deepened and she let her body mold against his as he wrapped his arms about her. Exactly as she'd guessed, it felt like being hugged by a big, warm, kindly bear. His powerful hands were gentle as they held her close.

She'd become enthralled with watching him work in his

kitchen—his chocolate shop—even if it was just designing. The focus, the obvious joy he took in the process. His quick smile and bright eyes had gone quiet as he worked and she could see the man revealed. He gave a first (and second and third) impression of being light-hearted and quick-thinking, living for the banter of the moment.

But not when he was working on a chocolate recipe. To that he brought a focus she easily recognized: it was the difference of a grunt in for a tour or two and the long-term professional soldier.

And at the moment, he was bringing that same incredible intensity of concentration to melting her bones as if they were actually made of chocolate.

It was working.

Not only was he reshaping her body to his, but if he were suddenly to let go, her liquid knees would be sure to melt out from under her.

He didn't let her go, but he did ease back and break their kiss by the simple expedient of standing up straight. He had at least eight inches on her height...she'd never kissed such a tall man. Rather than uncomfortably submissive, she felt as if she was being cared for. The former she'd have to think about but the latter she had no experience with and it was confusing as hell.

"Now," he whispered as he looked down at her with those deep, warm eyes of his. "Why are you here?"

"This," she managed on an uneasy breath that didn't sound anything like her.

"Not good enough, Linda."

Not good enough? If his kiss and embrace had felt any better she'd—

Again Clive left her with no good words.

"What are you really asking, Clive?"

"We're not going to simply tumble into bed and screw each other's brains out."

"We're not?" That sounded very good at the moment.

"Linda," he practically groaned in agony.

Unable to think while looking at his eyes, she tipped her head down and placed her nose and forehead against his chest.

With his strong hands he dug into her back muscles and continued the job of melting her against him.

If they weren't here to screw... But they were. She knew enough about reading men to know that's exactly why they were here. It was why she'd said he should take her home and he hadn't argued. At least not until now when the bedroom door stood less than ten feet away. Hell of a time to stop a seduction.

Unless that's what this was. Was it?

Instead of a hot, sweaty release, what if... What if... What if she actually *wanted* to be here? To be here with Clive rather than just some guy most likely to sate her body for a night?

And it was true.

Dilya had whispered something offhand before she left the Chocolate Shop. They'd been looking down at the two dogs, and Zackie was actually sitting at alert and waiting quietly for the next command. "Such a good doggie. We can see so much more of who you are when you're being quiet, can't we?" The dog had wagged her tail in happy response, revealing that she really was a sweetheart and not just a hyperactive ball of beautiful fur.

Then Dilya had been gone, leaving Linda to watch the quietly working Clive.

And she'd seen so much more of who he was. He was a man alive with ideas. His chocolate shop had photos of them taped to every surface: a mottled orange-and-red sky, a breaking ocean wave, a red-winged blackbird's wing. He didn't merely make chocolates. Clive sought inspiration in nature. He might look like the guy most likely to play the front four on a football team, but instead she could only marvel at the delicate confections he'd created and the way he drew. Beneath that ever-so-distracting exterior, there was an intelligent, thoughtful, and skilled man.

At that moment, his probing fingers found a locked-up muscle beneath her right shoulder blade. He massaged it until it released with a suddenness that took her breath away. And when she breathed back in, with her face still planted against his chest, he filled her senses just as surely as he'd filled her thoughts.

She now knew why she was here.

"Take me to bed, Clive." She'd thought it would be the action that mattered. But it wasn't. It was the man.

———

IT WAS ENOUGH.

It was too much.

Clive ached for Linda like he'd ached for no woman before.

He'd wanted her clear words that she really did want to be here. That she did want to give her body to him.

And she certainly didn't need to tell him twice.

He scooped her up in his arms, and she simply buried her face against his neck. Turning sideways, he barely managed to scoot them through the bedroom door.

Then, by the light spilling in through the doorway, he saw that the bed was unmade. His bathrobe was on the floor. The…

He hadn't known he'd be bringing home a beautiful woman or he'd have—

Linda looked up to see why he'd stopped.

"You really are a civilian. As long as those rumples are all yours, you'll get no complaints from me."

"They're all mine," his voice felt hoarse, stuck deep in his chest. "Have been for a while." Longer than usual, by far. As if he'd somehow known he was waiting for Linda Hamlin to step into his life.

She offered a thoughtful hum that might have been pleasure and might have been a cat's purr of contentment.

He was past thinking about such things. Setting her on her feet, he wasn't really sure how to begin. But Linda had taken care of that without him noticing. As he'd carried her, she'd unbuttoned his shirt.

Once again she placed her face against his chest; he now felt the tickle of her warm breath on his skin. The brush of her impossibly soft hair, even her happy sigh as she slid her arms inside his shirt until they were wrapped around him.

He wanted her to speak, though he wasn't sure why. Usually, when he bedded a woman, it was all about feeling: his hands on her skin, her reactions as he laved her body with touch and kiss as fine as decorating a chocolate. They would occasionally talk or guide and that was fine.

But with Linda, he wanted to hear her thoughts. He'd already learned that she was a woman of few words. He would have to coax her verbal responses just as he might another woman's physical ones.

"Tell me about—" his words choked off as she slipped his pants and underwear off his hips and dragged his bare body against her with fingers dug hard into his behind. She was so distracting that again he hadn't noticed her actions undressing him.

Undressing him. But she was still fully clothed. She hadn't even taken off her US Secret Service jacket, though she had unzipped it when they'd entered the apartment building.

US Secret Service. His past was filled with secretaries, aides, a lobbyist or two, and even a US Congresswoman. All professional women of the office variety. And, in hindsight, a disproportionate number of them had indeed been tall blondes exactly as Linda had teased him.

This short brunette of the military variety was something completely new.

Linda took a step back and shucked off her jacket. He almost missed the fact that if he didn't stop her, she'd strip down the rest of the way just as quickly.

He wanted her naked, but not merely stripped down.

Grabbing one of her hands before it could grab the hem of her blouse, he went to twirl her into an impromptu dance step.

Except his pants had slid from around his thighs to around his ankles and instead of stepping forward into the lead, he plunged to the carpet, nearly crushing Thor, who had come in to see what was going on. With a yip of surprise, Thor scooted back out the bedroom door.

A similar sound came from Linda because he hadn't let go of her hand as he went down. She landed hard against him, firmly planting a shoulder in his gut and knocking most of the wind out of him.

While he was busy gasping for air like a beached fish, Linda propped an elbow on his ribs and looked down at him.

"Is this how you usually run your seductions?"

"Sure," he managed on a gasp. "Dark choco-late," took two breaths. "Smooth moves. Wrestle to carpet." He tried to reach for her, but his arms were still in his shirtsleeves and the bulk of the shirt was pinned beneath him. *Worst seduction, ever.*

Then Linda did what he'd been trying to forestall, or at least draw out. She grabbed the back collar of her blouse, yanked it off, then tossed it aside. A slightly stained gray sports bra followed moments later.

He'd been right. With Linda Hamlin, you got what you saw. No lacy lingerie purchased special for the moment. No coyness over wearing work clothes—no matter how high end—rather than date clothes.

And with absolutely spectacular results. He knew of her strength. Had witnessed it, felt it as he'd rubbed her back. But to see how so much power had been translated into the female form was astonishing. She looked only a little broader of shoulder than might be expected for her size. But with even the slightest motion, he could see the muscles rippling beneath her beautiful skin.

And what skin. It wasn't all smooth, powdered, moisturized,

and who knew what else. There were scars on her arms, a big one on her shoulder that looked like...

"Dog teeth?"

She followed the line of his gaze, then shrugged. "Bite training. He caught me above the training sleeve. Seventeen stitches. I thought men only looked at one thing on naked women."

"Well, I'll admit to noting that you have exceptionally nice breasts." Again he reached for them and again he failed. He tried to raise his shoulders enough to free the trapped shirt, but she was still leaning against his chest and he couldn't get the leverage.

But Linda was about so much more than her womanly parts. Though now that she'd mentioned them, it *was* hard to look away.

That earned him a smile before she leaned down and rubbed against him chest-to-chest. He watched her eyes as she slowly gave herself over to the sensations. The tough soldier-turned-dog handler faded away and the hidden woman who intrigued him as much as the latter slowly emerged. Her eyes slid shut and her mouth opened slightly as the shift continued.

He leaned up enough to kiss her and they both groaned.

"Where?" She finally whispered.

Clive waved a hand at the nearby nightstand. She straddled his chest, still wearing her khakis as she reached over and dug out some protection. He planted a kiss on her breastbone just between her breasts and she scooped a hand to support his head and keep it there. Her breasts were soft and warm, brushing against his cheeks. He'd always been an unabashed breast man, in any size. But at her breastbone he felt as if he was somehow closer to who she was. Powerful muscle close over solid bone. The essence of this woman lay not in her splendid curves, but in her pervasive inner and outer strength.

With him sheathed and her pants shed, again in some maneuver he'd missed, she hovered over him. Her palms braced on his shoulders kept him still trapped by his shirt. Pinned by that and the most dramatic woman he'd ever been with.

LINDA FELT as if she teetered upon some brink. Men were easy. You gave them what they wanted and, if all went well, you got some of what you wanted as well.

But Clive confused her.

He kept insisting on seeing *her*, Linda, rather than merely some woman. And if she knew who that was, it would definitely help.

She knew Sergeant Hamlin. More than one unit had nicknamed her Ball-breaker because she didn't take shit from anyone. And any grunt who dared perform at one millimeter less than a hundred percent of their potential around her soon found out just how dangerous that was—though she saved literal ball-breaking just for those who didn't understand the meaning of the word *no*.

Clive had kissed right her where her dog tags had hung for a decade, as if he could somehow fill the hole that their removal had left. She didn't believe in nostalgia and had stripped them off as she'd driven out of the Fort Benning gates on that last day, but she'd missed them. Missed them horribly without realizing it until Clive planted a kiss there as if he could heal the gaping wound left by the removal of her dog tags and the end of her military career.

With a subtlety of understanding, he also didn't reach for her, merely letting his hands rest on her thighs where she knelt over him. He somehow knew that she had to find her own way through the maelstrom that being with him had stirred awake.

Men were *supposed* to be easy.

Clive Andrews *looked* easy. His sweet face and smiling eyes said that he absolutely *was* easy. But with every gesture, with every move, he proved that he was the most complex man she'd ever met.

His kindness was without question.

His humor, his ability to laugh at himself even as he tumbled to the carpet in the middle of a dance step and played the fool, was something she knew she'd be a better person if she could learn.

And the man... There wasn't a thing about him that wasn't substantial.

His impact on her thoughts was all out of proportion with any prior assignation. And to take him inside... It felt as if she was about to bare her very soul for him to see. Of course, Clive Andrews was the one proving to her that she even *had* a soul, so perhaps that wasn't a bad thing.

Easing down, she slowly took him in. One long, slow, delicious slide all the way down until she couldn't believe how extraordinarily he filled her in every way.

Definitely not a bad thing.

"IT WILL BE DAWN SOON," Linda mumbled from where she lay beneath the covers, her head on his chest.

"Dawn," Clive managed to acknowledge as he finger-brushed her hair so that it spread like a liquid ganache over his neck and shoulders. A featherweight as light as her kisses and the flutter of her eyelashes against his cheek when they kissed.

Dawn of a new day. New day? He had trouble even remembering the Clive of yesterday. In a single night, Linda Hamlin had transformed him. Yesterday he'd been a chocolatier who enjoyed women. Today he knew for a fact that there was no other woman for him.

He couldn't remember the last time he'd been awake a whole night and come out of it feeling more energized than when the evening had started. Yes, sex on the carpet, hard against the tile wall in the shower with the hot water sluicing over them, and finally on top of her in the bed had certainly had their impact. But it was the times between, curled up in each other's arms and talking easily, that he'd most remember.

Piece by tiny piece, like a layered chocolate truffle that continued without end, she slowly revealed herself. The triumphs and heartbreaks of working with the dogs. And with the people. He'd never given much thought to the civilians of countries caught up in war zones against their wishes. Now they seemed so real that he'd never see the war-torn, ex-military men prowling along the White House fence the same way again. They hadn't wanted war either, but everything had been stripped from them until all they had left was looking through an iron fence at the center of power. Did they find comfort there or a focus for their ire?

And he was a chocolatier. How useless was that?

Yet Linda was so compassionate that she had talked him down from that as well. "It gives me hope, knowing that normal life continues. That I can walk into the mall and hit See's Candies. It's a sign of all the things we're doing right." After that he'd made a particularly gentle love to her, for it was the best way he could think to thank her.

"I just wish I could do more," he brushed at her hair some more. Out the window, the low gray clouds reflected back the streetlights.

"You do." She pulled back the sheets enough to uncover her face so that he could trace his fingertips over her fine features. Somehow she knew that it was the same conversation they'd abandoned hours before. "Think about the dessert you just designed."

He'd told her about it earlier. Now it sounded trite. He rolled his eyes.

"No, Clive," she propped herself up to look down at him. "I'm serious. A mission isn't achieved by me and my dog leading the way, searching for IEDs. It's won by the intel analyst who found the target, the commander who planned and ordered the raid. The helo pilots. The grunts on the ground. The snipers on overwatch. The eyes in the sky of the drone operators. We each do our little piece. Even then victory isn't assured, but it's not for want of trying."

Clive blinked at the force of her tirade, but she continued.

"Your role may not seem obvious to you, but how do you know that your contribution won't be the tipping point? You don't. You just do what every good soldier does. You do the best you can; and as long as you keep doing that, no one can ask more of you. Besides, you're much farther up the chain than I am. Maybe your 'silly' dessert will help make a change so that people like me don't have to deploy in the first place."

"Have you always been such an optimist?"

"I'm not. I'm a fierce pessimist. Maybe I'll tell you about my parents someday."

Then she shuddered against him and he wasn't so sure that she was pretending. Only then did he realize that her life story to him had begun with the moment she joined the Army.

"Or maybe not," she continued softly. "But I'm also a realist who see what works."

"There must be something you're optimistic about?"

In answer she slid a hand down his chest, over his stomach, and wrapped those fine fingers around him.

"Okay," he had to agree. "I'm feeling rather optimistic about that too."

CHAPTER EIGHT

*P*erimeter patrol. It felt good to be outdoors for a change.

Even if it was snowing. She was in such a good mood that the light snowfall looked pretty. If it persisted through the day and the temperature didn't rise, she'd probably be less enamored by this afternoon. For now, it was pleasant. Each cool snowflake that landed on her face and melted seemed to freeze and wash clean an old memory leaving only the fresh and new ones behind.

Linda also appreciated having a tall fence *between* her and the White House for a change. Between her and Clive.

She'd pay for the lack of sleep later, though the Rangers had taught her to go two or three days without when needed. But she'd never felt more awake rather than less with the passage of time.

Clive had slipped past her guard. She wasn't used to guys spending the night. In all fairness, she'd been in his apartment, so it would have been up to her to leave. But she hadn't even thought about it. Two a.m. had slipped by just as pleasantly as their predawn tussle in the sheets. She was comfortable in his arms like no other's before. Which was unnerving enough to confuse the crap out of her.

Then this morning he'd given her a pair of gloves that he'd knit for his mother, but she'd died before he'd finished them.

"They were to be our cribbage gloves."

She'd inspected them carefully. Rows and rows of tiny beer glasses, some amber, some stout brown, and each with a white foam cap. "They look like drinking gloves."

"We used to go to a pub together to have a beer and play cribbage." Then he'd folded down the thumb. Sure enough, on the inside face of it was a tiny cribbage board.

Even now she felt the kiss on each palm before he'd slipped the gloves on her hands.

Clive hadn't just slipped past her guard—he'd blown by it as if it wasn't even there.

This morning, an officer named Claremont was following her along the fence line, but far enough back that she didn't have to interact with him. His job was two-fold: to act as backup if Thor found anything and to answer questions about Thor so that they could keep moving and do their job. She could hear him behind her.

"Yes, he's really a Secret Service dog."

"No, you can't pet him. Sorry."

"Yes, he may look silly, but his nose is one of the top ones in the business."

"His breed, ma'am? Pure mutt."

"Yes, he's the one who caught the bomber yesterday."

"No. He's at work right now, so he can't stop for pictures, sir."

He was repeating the last two so often that it was making Linda crazy. Thor had become an overnight celebrity. The Secret Service was generally very careful to keep quiet just how many lunatics they quietly nabbed at the fence line carrying explosives.

But the diplomat, by dropping his briefcase in the center of Lafayette Square, had turned it into a front page spectacle—below the fold, but still front page. With a big close-up of Thor. The hero dog had drawn crowds of his own to the White House fence.

Well, the public weren't the only ones who now knew who she was. The other dog handlers circling the fence offered her a nod of greeting, even the ones she'd never seen before. Outside the line, she and another floppy-eared were on opposite rotations, so they passed one another each half-rotation around the White House grounds. Even from inside the fence line, the handlers with the Malinois ERTs—Emergency Response Team dogs—nodded a greeting.

She missed the prestige of handling a Malinois war dog. They were fierce and fiercely loyal. They could also be utterly charming, but they were always impressive. Yet Thor, the least impressive dog on the entire team, had a sweetness that went all the way to his core.

And they were finding a place for themselves. She'd burned out in the Rangers. Witnessing so much death and suffering had taken its toll. But Linda had stayed an extra two-year tour just because she had no idea where she could possibly belong outside of the Army. But maybe, just maybe, she was finding it.

"You're famous," a voice whispered close beside her.

Linda prepared herself to actually deal with a tourist when she recognized the voice. "Good morning, Dilya."

The girl was dressed in a massive parka of neon blue that almost reached her knees. She wore a knit hat of blue with gold stripes with a tail so long that she had the end tied around her throat as a scarf. She existed only from her brilliant green eyes to her lower lip.

"Is that hat-scarf thing Clive's doing? *Gute Hund,*" she told Thor so that he could take a moment to greet Dilya and pee on a handy lamppost.

Dilya nodded.

"Where's Zackie?"

"I didn't want to distract Thor. Besides, I'm not supposed to take her off the grounds. It's weird how many people want to kidnap the First Dog."

It was weird, but she'd seen the statistics on threats against White House pets. More than one tour guest had tried to smuggle a First Cat out under their coats. "Good choice. We've got to get back to work, but you're welcome to walk with us. Thor, *Such.*" And once more he was back on the job, sniffing the air as he moved through the crowds gawking at the White House. Whenever someone stepped too far aside, as if perhaps shifting to avoid being smelled by Thor, she'd twitch his leash ever so slightly and he'd shift over to check them.

Dilya fell in close beside her. With a neat awareness, she stayed an extra half step to the side so that she wouldn't be in the way if Linda had to react.

"Did you get any more training done?"

"No, she's with the First Lady over in the East Wing. They're usually good together for the morning. After lunch she's off to New York."

Meeting at the UN, Linda recalled from the morning briefing. The President was scheduled to be inside all day.

"I'm usually at school in the mornings anyway."

"Why aren't you today?"

"Saturday. Duh!"

"Oh," Linda had completely lost track of the days. She simply checked the duty roster at checkout each evening to see if she was on or off the following day.

"Is that where you caught him?" They were passing Lafayette Square.

"Yes. Close by the Andrew Jackson statue in the center. Though Thor picked up his trail three blocks that way."

Dilya was looking from the statue to along G Street.

She did it enough times that Linda finally had to ask what she was thinking.

"Well…" she drew it out. "He wasn't really headed anywhere,

was he. Not to Hay-Adams Hotel or he would have crossed the square on the other side of the statue. And not toward Blair House where the Japanese ambassador was meeting with their prime minister or he wouldn't have come into the square at all."

An observation that had been brought up at yesterday's debriefing, but no one knew how to interpret.

"But by walking along G Street, he was almost asking to be found. If you hadn't caught him, I wonder if he would have kept walking back and forth."

Linda froze, earning her a puzzled look from Thor. She looked up the street, imagining a map of DC in her mind. Three blocks to the Metro Center subway station. Two blocks and a block left beyond that to the Secret Service Headquarters building. It would be perhaps the *most* patrolled approach to the White House just for that reason.

Dilya continued her speculation, "I mean, if I was going to smuggle four kilos of explosives into the vicinity of the White House without a dog catching me, that isn't a route I would have followed. Combine that with a diplomatic pass and something isn't right."

"How did you know it was four kilos?" The fact of the diplomatic pass had also been kept out of the papers, yet somehow Dilya knew.

Linda didn't wait for the girl to answer. She keyed the radio mic clipped to her shoulder. "Sergeant Hamlin for Captain Baxter."

"Baxter here."

"What if the bomber *wanted* to be caught?"

There was a long silence. Then, "Get your ass in here. I'll send another team out to patrol the line."

She acknowledged and turned to thank Dilya, but she was gone. Even her neon blue parka and matching hat were nowhere to be seen.

IT TOOK Clive most of the day to perfect the dessert for the State Dinner. Chef Klaus liked it well enough, even if he didn't understand the higher concept. First Lady Anne Darlington-Thomas understood it the moment she saw it and was then delighted with the taste. She looked absolutely elegant and had a small entourage in tow that crowded his tiny shop badly.

"You've outdone yourself, Chef Andrews." The First Lady began handing around his Pocky-stick treats to the rest of the gathering.

"Thank you, ma'am."

An assistant stood by her side with a tablet at the ready for notetaking. The White House photographer was maneuvering for a good photo—thankfully the assistant had called ahead and he'd had time to don a fresh apron and set out his creations for the State Dinner in a neat display. Still the photograph was a challenge because the First Lady was even shorter than Linda and didn't reach his shoulder. Special Agent Detra Willand, a shapely and cheery blonde in charge of the First Lady's protection detail, smiled brightly at the contrast as she stood guard in the doorway.

Dilya slipped in quietly, leading Zackie, and took one as well.

"Yum!" Dilya broke off part of the bare biscuit and fed it to the dog. " I one heard someone say that life is uncertain…"

"…*so eat dessert first.*" Clive and the First Lady spoke in unison. Then the First Lady looked thoughtful.

"Chef Andrews, can you scale these down and serve them as a treat at the predinner reception?"

Clive considered. Yes, he could scale them down now that he had the techniques figured out. But then he'd need a suitable dessert for the dinner. Perhaps Jacques Torres' chocolate soup might have a place after all. Made of the same dark chocolate, perhaps with a passionfruit-flavored meringue. Each bowl accompanied by a single one of his scaled-up version of a twirled chocolate Pocky stick. For those who had snacked on the smaller ones at the reception, it would bring the concept full circle, emphasizing the unity of the evening.

When he laid out the idea, the First Lady had practically glowed with appreciation.

"You are thinking at a whole new level, Chef Andrews. I like that."

"I had someone offer me..." *her body and her passion* "...some clear insights."

"Oh, I do so *love* those kinds of insights." She breezed out of the kitchen with her entourage hurrying close on her heels. Dilya grinned at him, clearly not missing a thing, then took another stick of chocolate and followed the First Lady as well—Zackie's claws ticking brightly on the linoleum floor.

He could only gape after her. What was it with women? Did they simply assume that all good bounty flowed directly from them? Even if the First Lady was absolutely right in this case.

All good bounty? Who was he kidding?

He'd known Linda Hamlin for mere days and if she was willing to promise the rest of her life with him, he'd go down on bent knee right here and now in his chocolate shop. How was a sane man ever supposed to get enough of someone like her?

Well, that one he knew how to answer. The only way to get enough was to indeed commit to a lifetime together. That was the only way there would ever be enough time.

The fact that the thought was completely and certifiably insane wasn't bothering him as much as he'd expect it to. Is this what being in love was?

If love was like a chocolate, what would it be?

He wasn't sure, but he began pulling out his favorite ingredients. Rather than an ultra-high-end chocolate, he selected a Lindt couverture. It offered a taste of homey familiarity rather than a unique experience for the palate. Apricot liquor. Dried Bing cherries that he'd candy in an apricot nectar simple syrup. A sprinkle of candied ginger on a red chocolate surface. Then—

He looked at it all on the counter and knew it was wrong.

Yes, it would make a nice chocolate. But it would be about him and what he liked. He wanted it to be about Linda. Even better, he wanted it to be about them.

Once more Clive studied the ingredients on the counter. Then the ones in his pantry.

The problem was that he didn't know enough about *her*. He knew how she made him feel—like the luckiest chef on the planet. No other woman could ever offer that incredible blend of strength and surety and clarity.

But he couldn't think of how to make a chocolate out of those words.

And what words would she use?

He didn't know. Her thoughts were like the hidden center of a treat—unknown except to the baker until they were bitten into. There was no secret code worked into the finishing decoration to tell him what she had contained within.

Clive might not know her, but he couldn't deny being fascinated.

Fascinated?

Completely gone. He simply knew she was the right woman for him.

Again the thought seemed crazy, but it was as right as that first moment he'd bitten into couverture chocolate and the future had opened up for him.

Linda Hamlin was the one for him.

Now, how to go about finding more about who she actually was and convincing her that he was the one for her.

"YOU *WHAT?*" Linda's body ignored her shock and kept doing what it had been doing.

She and Clive were right in the middle of another night's research into just how good it was possible to make each other feel—when he'd mumbled out those three impossible words.

"Tell me. I didn't just hear. What I just heard." It took her three gasping breaths to get the sentence out.

Clive offered one of his uncomfortable shrugs. He opened his mouth, but she cut him off.

"And don't spout anything. About George Washington. Not telling lies!" Her pulse rate was still escalating, just not for the reasons it should be.

He closed his mouth again.

"This isn't happening." She straddled over him in his big Barcalounger. It was tipped back just enough that his incredible hands had access to her chest and the wonderful things he'd proven he could do there.

"Sorry," he whispered.

Release was so close, for both of them. She'd learned to read his gasping breaths and clenching thighs to know just how close.

And then he'd said...

She couldn't even think it.

But they were so close that even the least movement...

Her body, out of her control, sank down hard one last time and the waves hammered through her, stealing the last of her breath and mind. Moments later, the pulses wracking her own body tipped Clive off the edge as well.

"So good," was all she could mumble. "So good." Sex with Clive was better than any prior experience had even hinted was possible.

He held her hips tight against his as they rode it out together. Every shudder, every breath—she could feel every nuance through his physical connection deep inside her where he was plugged directly in her nervous system.

When at last their shared body had quieted, she tipped her forehead against his. "It's okay, Clive. It's just something that guys are dumb enough to say during sex. They think that sex equals love and spout things out. Sorry I yelled, I get that."

But resting brow-to-brow, she could feel him shaking his head.

"Do *not* repeat it!"

"Okay," he whispered.

"God damn it, Clive!" Linda pushed back to glare down at him. "There's no such thing, outside of fairy tales and Hollywood movies. You do know that, right? Who the hell am I kidding? You're a guy who knits and makes chocolate for a living. You believe in the Easter Bunny, the Tooth Fairy, and true love."

"Well, I kind of outgrew the Tooth Fairy—she didn't like me much because I'm a chocolatier. I'm totally in good with the Easter Bunny, though. I'm a big fan. Huge."

"Clive," her groan felt like it was made of shards of glass. "We've known each other for maybe three days."

"Six, actually. It's past midnight."

"Clive!"

He ran his hands up her bare back and pulled her in.

She resisted. Well, she *wanted* to resist, but she knew how good it felt to lie against him. And knew just how perfectly he could hold her with those big, wonderful hands of his. Her traitorous body leaned in against him until they were chest to chest and she could rest her head on his shoulder.

"How can you believe in love?"

"How can you not?"

Linda buried her face against his neck and sure enough, his hands sliding up and down his back soothed her. But she didn't want to be soothed. She didn't want to fall into some male-engineered trap.

"No," she pushed back up. "No!" She extricated herself from Clive and his goddamn chair. Because it was tipped partway back, the angles were all wrong, but she finally managed to obtain enough leverage to stand to the side and look down at him. He was *so* beautiful. So fantastically male.

He was also a dangerous drug. She'd felt less effect from morphine ampoules delivered from field medkits when she'd been injured. The potency of Clive Andrews wasn't merely a force to be reckoned with. For a moment there, she'd almost fallen under his spell.

But no!

She *knew* better.

They always said that if you didn't know what to respond when the other person said those three awful words, then that was the answer.

But she knew exactly what to say.

"Clive. I *don't* love you." Then she couldn't stop herself. "You're a really great fuck," the best she'd ever had. "But that's all this is."

And he looked like she'd just rammed her battle knife under his ribcage.

She wanted to reach for him. Take his hand. Console him. But...she'd just forever forfeited that privilege with those four words of her own.

CLIVE COULDN'T LOOK at her, but he couldn't look away either. Naked, beautiful, her hair brushing her powerful shoulders. So strong and yet so angry.

He knew he shouldn't have said that he loved her. He knew it the instant the words had slipped out of his mouth. But they'd been so true. All of the way down to the core. It hadn't been something tossed out in the throes of passion, it had simply been clarified so perfectly in that instant. He knew its truth as surely as he knew his passion for chocolate.

And it wasn't merely how she felt, how she smelled, how she

tasted. Nothing had prepared him for the way she gave with all of her being. Her open heart and the connections she built so easily with Thor and Dilya—it had taken him months to win Dilya's trust and Linda had done it in minutes. Picturing Linda with children of her own was the easiest thing in the world. Picturing her with *their* children…

It had taken his breath away and the words had spilled out.

Saying those words aloud had been a shock to him as well, but they were nothing compared to her answer: *I don't love you.* He felt as if he'd been gutted and wished he could somehow curl up and hide rather than lie bonelessly sprawled back in his chair, unable to find the leverage to climb to his feet. Spread out like a corpse whose heart had just been hacked out of his chest, inspected, and found wanting.

Linda began dressing as efficiently as she did everything else and all he could do was watch.

"You're a wonderful man, Clive."

Socks and underwear.

"The best time I've ever had." As if he was a carnival ride.

Pants and belt.

"What you don't understand is that there's no such thing as love. It's just a delusion. A mass hallucination cooked up by Hollywood and romance authors."

She bent down to tie her boots, offering him an incredible view of her naked breasts partly masked by a fall of her luxurious hair.

"No!" He protested as her words sank in. "Wait. That's wrong. Of course love exists." He finally found the chair controls and tipped it upright enough for him to really face her.

"No." Bra, blouse, fleece vest. "It's a stupid word for a cruel concept that is used only to hurt and manipulate."

Shoulder holster, sidearm, and taser.

"Linda, you can't believe—"

"I *don't* believe." USSS jacket. "I *know.*"

Her face was cold, expressionless. This wasn't the woman...or even the soldier. She'd gone somewhere far beyond either of those.

"Love is an empty word said by a husband to his wife before he goes off to screw another coed. It the word a mother uses to manipulate and guilt-trip her child: *If you loved me, you'd...* The song is right. Love isn't a weapon, it's a goddamn battlefield."

A snap of her fingers and Thor trotted to her side.

She pulled out the gloves he given her—his mother's cribbage gloves. She rubbed a thumb over them for a moment, then set them on the coffee table beside the last of the pizza he'd made for her.

"Goodbye, Clive."

"Wait! Let's talk—" But she was gone, with Thor at her heels.

The door swung softly shut.

Leaving him to sit naked and alone.

LINDA DIDN'T TAKE the Metro.

She needed to walk it off.

Hot tracks scored her cold cheeks like the razor slice of flying shrapnel—momentary surprise, and then, after a pause just long enough to think you were lucky and had escaped this time, the slicing pain. She hadn't cried since...

She remembered the day perfectly while she strode blindly down Wisconsin Avenue. It was a good thing it was two in the morning and there was no traffic. She couldn't seem to stop herself as she strode through intersection after intersection no matter what the lights were doing.

A young girl. The day before she'd turned eleven. She could still see it with crystalline clarity in her mind's eye—sharper than the night's fluttering snow caught in successive streetlamps.

Standing outside her parents' open bedroom door. Her best friend beside her. Home from school for a play date.

Everyone always talked about how wonderful and kind her parents were. What great hosts. The joy of every party. So helpful.

But that wasn't what she and Peggy saw.

Her parents. Toe to toe in the bedroom. Screaming at each other as if they were ready to commit murder.

She recalled the images like snapshots: the rumpled bed, her father naked, a blonde college student that Father had said he was tutoring cowered in the corner trying to hide her own nakedness, her mother raging.

The words had tumbled by her, barely recognized, not understood until later: cheating fuck, icy bitch, limp-dicked loser, dried-out hag with nothing but a dusty hole where all joy died…

But worse than the words had been when they'd turned and noticed their audience.

Her father had merely sworn, "There's the other useless bitch. Why the hell did we ever have a kid?"

Her mother hadn't corrected him. Hadn't defended her. Instead she'd stridden to the door in her Armani power pantsuit and whispered harshly, "Neither of you little shits saw or heard a thing!" Then she'd slammed the door in their faces.

Peggy hadn't been there when Linda had finally recovered. Her pinkie-sworn, best-friend-forever never spoke to her again. Word got around, and not many of their classmates ever had either. Linda's eleventh birthday party, her last ever, had been attended by her golden retriever. That's what had driven her out of the social set and into sports, which had ultimately led her to the military. None of the jocks knew of the horror that was her parents. They didn't know she was now a social pariah. She never once took any of her sports friends to her house.

And that evening at dinner? Everyone just pretended that nothing had happened, including her. Her father still tutored his students at the house, often in the bedroom, sometimes more than one at a time. Her mother rarely came home from Montpelier—except when there were dinners or parties to host, of course. When Linda visited there, her mother was always with a different man—whoever's political favors she was currying at the time. Linda had spent all of her accumulated allowance to buy top-quality noise-canceling headphones—the only possession she never forgot to take from place to place.

It wasn't the night of the fight that Linda had last cried. She'd just kept her dry-eyed face buried in Beau's fur as she and her dog hid together in her bedroom closet.

When the aged golden retriever had died two months later, *that* was when it all came out. She'd cried so hard that they'd had to call the paramedics and give her a muscle relaxant before she could stop.

That had been her very last time.

Until now.

Dammit!

She wiped at her eyes with chilled fingers, all the colder as they were soaked in salt water.

A lone passerby hesitated as if he might offer to help—then hurried away fast. Smart man.

Wisconsin intersected Massachusetts. Dupont Circle sent her south along Connecticut. Until once more she stood in Lafayette Square with the White House shining like a beacon. A lone dog team patrolled along Pennsylvania. Emergency response dogs would be in their ERT vans—one of them was bound to have spotted her and was keeping an eye on her just in case.

Warning: Crazy bitch in Lafayette Square at three a.m. Alert the QRT!

In her current mood she was half tempted to do something that would get a Quick Response Team to come and put her out of her misery. How could she have done that to Clive? He *was* the best fuck of her life, but there'd been no reason to say it that way.

She brushed the thin coating of snow off a bench and sat. Thor settled at her feet. Linda cursed herself as she gathered him into her arms.

"Oh, I'm so sorry, buddy. I just made you walk five miles." She buried her face in his fur as he tried to lick the dried salt from her face. Even without his lead clipped on, he'd stuck with her.

A dog. That was all a woman could trust. Her own self and her dog.

Then she remembered the devastated look on Clive's face as she carved up his heart and fed it back to him.

She'd sworn that she'd never be cruel like her parents, but now that rule lay shattered with a direct hit. Apparently cruelty wasn't a choice, it was genetic.

Maybe not so much with trusting herself.

Thor finished cleaning her face and began on his own paws.

Okay. At least she could trust her dog.

CHAPTER NINE

"*A* difficult night, my dear?" A homeless woman settled on the bench beside Linda.

"Could you just leave me alone?"

"Oh no. I don't think that's a good idea at all, dearie." Then the woman held out a dog biscuit.

Linda yanked Thor away before he could even sniff it. MWDs often carried ten or even twenty thousand dollar bounties on their heads in war zones—fifty times the average per capita yearly income in Afghanistan. She'd never heard of anyone poisoning a Secret Service dog, but Thor was not going to be the first.

She reached for her taser, even as it sank in that the voice was familiar. A clump of silver hair spilled out of the tattered hood of the woman's knit sweater and caught the streetlight. Bright blue eyes watched her intently.

"Miss Watson." Dressed like a bag lady, complete with a couple of badly scuffed plastic bags and wearing enough layers that she looked quite fat. Earlier she'd looked, well, it was hard to remember. Matronly? Without the voice, Linda never would have recognized her.

"You were expecting Greta Garbo?"

"Was she one of your spies?" Linda let loose her hold on Thor and Miss Watson once again offered the biscuit, which he happily took.

"She was before my time. The stories are very conflicted about her, just as everything else was."

"But…"

Miss Watson smiled. "Yes, she was deeply involved in very private ways—she did more than many in the fight against Hitler. Shall I repeat my question?"

"Please don't." She picked up some of the biscuit that Thor had broken off and dropped into her lap, holding it out for him to take once more.

"In that case, I will inquire as to the progress of your thinking about our would-be bomber."

"Is *nothing* secret in the White House?" Then Linda remembered who she was talking to and sighed. "My current, private theory is that he wasn't a bomber. The X-ray of the briefcase showed no signs of a trigger mechanism or timer. It did create the opportunity to pat down both of the diplomats and if they were hiding something like a trigger, it was well done."

"So, you have two men who carried four kilograms of explosive through an area well known to be patrolled by explosives detection dogs." Somehow Miss Watson knew about that observation as well, even if it hadn't shed any more light on the Secret Service's thinking—though Secretary of State Mallinson had poured forth a lecture that was equal parts conspiracy, xenophobia, and accusations of the Service's incompetence.

"Yes," Linda rubbed Thor's nose and received a freezing cold sneeze in her face as a reward. She sighed and wiped it away. "And yesterday I was able to trace them using the traffic and surveillance camera feeds backward from where I picked up their trail. They didn't ride the Metro, instead merely passing it. They had indeed walked directly past the Secret Service Headquarters building. We spotted them emerging from a cab. We managed to trace them backward through two more cab rides—all three were short, within the city limits. Prior to that, their trail disappears as if the film had been snipped."

"And your thoughts." Miss Watson didn't make it a question.

"My thoughts?" Linda's thoughts were that if she could undo one thing in her life—any one thing—it wouldn't be her parents, it would be hurting Clive. But if ever she'd killed off something good so thoroughly that it could never recover, that was it. "I don't have any thoughts."

Miss Watson didn't even bother to scoff as she had during their first meeting in her basement office. Instead, she held her hands out for Thor to sniff to prove they were empty of any second biscuit. He sighed and laid his head on Linda's chest to go to sleep.

"My thoughts are... Someone just wants to mess with our heads. Tomorrow, next week, at some point, they're going to actually do something and this event was merely to lay down a false trail. But whether it is to Japan, China, or freaking Tajikistan, I have no idea."

"Oh dear," Miss Watson said as daintily as a British mum about to serve tea and confronted by poorly cut cucumber sandwiches.

It was only then that Linda wondered if she'd actually been cleared to tell that information. The fact that Miss Watson somehow had an office in the subbasement of the White House— a clandestine one of long standing—said volumes about what she could do. But Linda had no spycraft of her own to estimate whether Miss Watson was good, bad, indifferent, crazy, or some sort of quadruple agent.

"I had rather feared that. However, I suspect that it will be far sooner than a week from now."

Linda swiveled to look at her more closely. "What do you know that I don't?"

Miss Watson's smile was rich with innuendo and an unlikely humor considering the situation.

"Ha. Ha. Ha. I meant about this situation."

"I know about a certain chef who has just arrived at the White House at an unprecedented hour by his standards. As to the other…" She reached out and squeezed Linda's hand with a very surprising strength, enough to dispel the frail, old woman persona. But she didn't speak.

Linda couldn't think about Clive being in the building shining right in front of her. Too close. Too real. So she set it aside.

But what did Miss Watson know? *Far sooner than a week from now.*

The pieces weren't connecting yet: a block of C-4 without being a bomb, a Japanese diplomat without being a Japanese diplomat, a flight for two to China as the first leg of a trip that would end who knew where.

Then she got it.

"It's not just *related* to the upcoming talks. It's *about* the upcoming meetings between Vietnam, Japan, and…" But even as she was saying it, she knew it was about something more.

It wouldn't be enough to merely disrupt the meetings—they'd just be held at a later date in another location.

However, if she wanted to permanently disrupt or damage the talks, or use them to showcase that no one was out of reach of whoever the true aggressor was, how would she go about it?

The meetings themselves? That wasn't very exciting. Horribly damaging, but missing that newsworthy hook. She worked with enough embedded war reporters to know they were always after the hottest hook. "What's the bin Laden-moment here?" always came out of their mouths at one time or another. Modern warfare was rarely about bin Laden-moments. It was about slow and steady attrition: one leader here, two weapon suppliers over there, a dozen fighters, an armored vehicle.

But if she was setting up a scenario specifically designed to *create* a bin Laden-media moment, she wouldn't do it during any dull meetings.

That left...the reception in the Residence and the State Dinner itself.

She swallowed hard. Both would require attacks *inside* the White House.

The State Dinner. Unless bipartisan slaughter was on the menu, it would be a hard situation to control. Would all of the potential targets even be at the same table?

That left the predinner reception on the Second Floor of the Residence.

"It's got to be—" Linda turned, but once again she and Thor were sitting alone in the center of Lafayette Square. She looked down at Thor.

"Between Miss Watson and Dilya, I really wish they'd stop doing that."

He offered a sleepy woof of commiseration.

CLIVE HAD CHASED LINDA. But by the time he'd dressed and raced out the door, she'd had too much of a head start and he didn't know where to begin looking for her.

He stood on the corner, slowly chilling down until he felt the ice form inside him as well as his freezing breath outside.

Everything had made such perfect sense just minutes before—a clarity of vision so clear that it felt prescient. He'd never believed in such things, though his mother had teased him about it often enough.

How did you know I was going to say that, Clive? Are you clairvoyant?

No. She'd simply said the same thing before when he'd done something equally stupid. He never forgot a word she said, even if he was slow to actually follow the advice. Which was too bad in retrospect—he'd eventually learned that most of Mom's advice had been good. He could use some of it now, but she'd died last spring. Her weak heart had made her so frail that the progression from cold to flu to pneumonia had been terrifyingly fast...and final. She'd died lying in a hospital bed clutching the cherry blossom scarf he'd knit for her, but she would never have a chance to wear. He'd buried it with her.

A passing thought that he wished she'd lived long enough to meet Linda just drove the knife in deeper.

And now as he stood in the freezing cold of the Washington, DC, night, he could feel the scars freshly opened.

No such thing as love.

She was wrong. He and his mother had had it—he still missed her as if she'd died yesterday. Maybe his father hadn't cared. He'd been at sea when she died and done no more than cashed the check for his share of her meager estate when he returned. He'd never even bothered to contact Clive. But that didn't negate that there was such a thing as love.

At a loss for what else to do, he'd entered the Metro and headed to work.

Now he stood in his kitchen and couldn't make sense of anything here either. The ingredients for a new dessert were still out on a prep table—the one that would be all about his heart. And his alone. He couldn't even see how the pieces fit together anymore.

He sat and put his head on the table.

What had he done wrong?

Fallen in love?

It was real. He could feel it like an agony in his chest, all curdled and sour, so he knew it was real.

But Linda didn't have a heart. He could see that now. Though he'd met few women like that, he knew men like that—his father for one.

And Clive thought he'd been so wise, so lucky. Able to recognize the woman who so rarely emerged from the soldier.

Now Clive understood that there was a reason she was a soldier.

Tonight he'd seen the other half of her. The part that made the soldier look kind and gentle. The woman who didn't merely deny love, but denied its existence. That *believed* it so deeply that she could say what she'd said.

She'd given him her body, but that was all. As if there weren't plenty of women willing to do that.

He raised his head enough to glare at the ingredients: Lindt dark couverture, apricot, ginger... His heart meant nothing to her. She'd just been using him for sex. Never in his life had he treated a woman that way. Even when it had just been purely physical, they'd both known that beforehand.

Not Linda. Her smile, her actions, her every breath had promised so much more. He'd seen the wonder on her face as she'd touched him. There was so much—

But there wasn't. Linda had made that perfectly clear.

He stood up and stowed the chocolate supplies back in his pantry. Then he began the long slow process of making the biscuit dough for the center of the dessert: reception nibbles for fifty, dessert for two hundred and forty.

CHAPTER TEN

*M*allinson had been in the Situation Room when she stuck her head in. He was quietly reviewing classified material for a change. They had a surprisingly pleasant discussion about her experiences overseas. He was an intelligent and insightful man, as long as she didn't mention the current situation.

So, at a loss for where else to go, Linda had once again crammed Special Agent Harvey Lieber into Captain Baxter's office, with Thor at her feet.

"What do you know that I don't?"

Lieber leaned back against a file cabinet with his arms crossed over his chest. "What are you talking about, Hamlin?"

"How did you know that the attack would be at tomorrow night's reception in the Residence?"

Both men flinched and looked at her aghast.

"You didn't know?"

They exchanged a quick glance, briefly suspicious of the other, before understanding that they were both in the dark. They *hadn't* known. But…

"Then why, the last time we met, did you ask if I could pass in a high-society environment if it wasn't to place me in that reception?"

Again that careful exchange of glances.

Linda considered the satisfaction of knocking their heads together versus her career having a future. She could feel that her nerves were frayed. She'd slept little the last two nights. The first night and a half because of Clive's splendid attentions and the last half because—she couldn't think about that.

"We have a source," Baxter began, then compressed his lips together.

"A very reliable one," Lieber acknowledged with equal reluctance.

"Let me guess, a woman in the basement."

"No." Again the dual blank look. "What woman? Which basement?"

Miss Watson. Subbasement Two, Mechanical Room 043. Librarian? Spy? Or something else entirely? Linda had no way to know Miss Watson's role, but something told her to keep that to herself. She held her silence until they got back on track.

Baxter finally rose to his feet, shoving Lieber aside, which almost pushed him into her lap because there was so little space. It was a good thing for Thor's sake that he was small enough to fit under her chair. Baxter unlocked the file cabinet, opened the top drawer, and then used a thumb print to open a safe mounted inside the drawer. He pulled out a slim folder with that same scary yellow-and-red fly sheet of an "Eyes Only" file. He handed it to her.

She opened it while the men reshuffled to their former positions.

Secure message.
From: WHPF
To: Captain Baxter

Cc: Senior Special Agent Lieber
Recommend immediate placement of Sergeant Hamlin
and dog Thor on internal White House patrol.
Level White protection.

IT WAS DATED the same day she'd passed the course at James J. Rowley Training Center.

"Who's WHPF?"

Lieber merely growled that it was Baxter's problem.

"We don't know. Something set up by the prior administration. We've learned that their advice is always good—and I mean always. But we have no idea who they are. They simply came online one day with a note from President Peter Matthews and Lieber's predecessor Frank Adams that said they had both personally certified the WHPF."

"Frank wouldn't tell me shit about who they were," and Agent Lieber's voice made it clear just how happy he *wasn't* about that. Then he held up his hands in resignation to the inevitable. "It stands for White House Protection Force and they've proven that they're good at it. Damned if I know where they get their information."

Linda could take a good guess. But maybe not. She remembered her two talks with Miss Watson. The matron was definitely in the loop, a piece of it, but last night in Lafayette Square she'd been reaching for answers as hard as Linda had. The simple memo in her hand spoke of a deep knowledge, or perhaps a broader reach than seemed likely from Mechanical Room 043.

"And Level White protection?"

Again the snarl from Lieber.

Baxter, on the other hand, actually smiled at his friend's upset expression. "It means that while you work for me, you've also been assigned undercover to the PPD."

Linda could feel the blood drain out of her face. The Presidential Protection Detail? Nobody got on that. It was the gold star times a thousand. Granted only after years of exceptional service.

"Wait! Undercover? Who else knows?"

Baxter, clearly enjoying his comrade's foul mood at having an undercover agent watching his own team, pointed a finger at the two of them. "Us and whoever the hell is behind the WHPF."

Linda couldn't speak. Couldn't think.

"We need a way to slip her in. Can't just put her there as an agent," Baxter pointed out.

Lieber looked her up and down with all the joy of inspecting a rotting piece of meat. "She and her dog as special guests for their fine work in Lafayette Square. Give Chief of Staff Cornelia Day a heads up. She'll alert the President and VP and get Hamlin on the guest list. Leak it to the press—they'll like a story about that. Do *not* reveal her true role."

"Of course not," Baxter shot back. She could hear the *Duh!* that Baxter didn't give voice to. She was starting to see the tight relationship between these two men. Their brotherly snarls back and forth would never be shown in public. But that they showed it in front of her made her wonder just *what* she'd suddenly stepped in the middle of.

Then she focused on what they'd just said. A special guest of the First Family? But she'd never met any of them.

"By the way, Hamlin," Lieber practically sneered at her. "Reception is tomorrow night. Can't wear your uniform if you're going undercover. You'd better go out and buy a dress."

CHAPTER ELEVEN

*B*y late afternoon, Linda was out of options. She could have slipped into the subbasement to ask Miss Watson, but she didn't want to risk intruding on Clive, even if his chocolate shop was two stories above her hidden office. That was too close and she just couldn't deal with it today.

There were no female agents on shift for her to ask, not that she really could now that she was spying on them.

In desperation, she finally had the White House operator track down Dilya for her. Unable to offer any explanations, she'd simply told the girl that she needed help buying a dress.

"Five minutes at the North Portico," Dilya sounded thrilled.

"Too soon. I have to take Thor back to the kennel at the Secret Service building first. Then I can—"

"No. No. No. You've gotta bring Thor, trust me. Make sure he wears his K-9 harness and stuff."

"And I suppose I should—" but the line had gone dead. Since she didn't have another jacket, and it was still cold out, she shrugged on her USSS one. Not exactly subtle, with the six-inch letters across the back, but there wasn't anything she could do about that. She considered leaving her weapons behind, but that felt wrong as well.

Dilya was there ahead of her.

"I can't take Thor into a department store."

"Sure you can. Service dog and like that." Dilya led the way down the driveway and toward the security gate.

"Maybe I should get dark glasses and a white cane too."

"If it makes you feel better. What kind of a dress?" She waved at the guards, who grinned back at her.

Linda blinked. Her thinking hadn't gone that far. Her last dress had been when she was fourteen for her mom's swearing-in ceremony as a state representative. She often wondered why such intelligent people as Vermonters kept reelecting her mother, but such things were beyond her.

"Um, a dressy dress?"

Dilya rolled her eyes.

"A dress I can afford."

"For a hot date with Chef Andrews?"

Linda's guard was down and the gut shot punched straight in.

"No," she somehow managed. Where was a medevac bird when she needed one? "Not for that," Linda struggled to hide her feelings.

"I like Chef Andrews," Dilya sounded defensive. So much for pretending it didn't hurt.

"I like him, too. It's not like I'm cheating on him." Not like that statement would ever have meaning anyway because she'd blown that all to hell just last night.

"Then what's the dress for?" Dilya had stopped in the middle of the closed stretch of Pennsylvania Avenue as if she was considering turning around and going back into the White House.

"I have to go to the reception and dinner tomorrow night in the Residence. I have to blend in."

"Ooo! Like undercover?"

"So much for keeping *that* a secret." This kid was going to be the death of her.

"Excellent! It's so cool. An agent gone undercover at a Residence reception."

Then a brief look crossed Dilya's face. Dark. Dangerous. This pretty young teen suddenly emanated a barely-contained fury. As she heard her own words, she looked ready to take on the fight herself. She glanced up at Linda.

"Are you good at what you do?"

Linda flashed an image of how thoroughly she'd eviscerated Clive, then did her best to set that aside. *Too good.* She could only nod.

"*Really* good? Protect-the-White-House kind of good?"

Linda considered how to answer that. "I guess I'd better be."

Dilya studied her a moment longer, then nodded sharply.

"Okay then." Her expression flipped back to being the pretty teen rather than the young woman ready to go to war. No. She remembered Clive's whispered comment, 'war orphan.' Dilya was ready to go *back* to war. "I've gotta get a nice dress too."

Linda wondered at the dual personality she'd just witnessed: Dilya's public persona and the fierce child-warrior beneath.

"Don't look at me like that," Dilya's expression saddened.

"Like what?"

"Like I'm an alien. I never killed anyone. I would have, but my new mom took care of that for me so I didn't have to." And she stated it like simple fact.

"Didn't have to?"

"Two men shot my real parents point-blank because we walked into the wrong place at the wrong time. Them I could have killed." There was no hint of doubt in her voice. "It made her sad, and I get why now. Back then I was too young to understand the price. Still I would have done it—they deserved to die."

A tone that Linda instantly recognized as having come from

her own mouth just this morning. *No such thing as love.* If she was so sure, then why did it hurt so much?

"Okay," Linda managed a breath, then remembering a long ago promise badly broken, she decided it was time to try trusting again. She held out a pinkie. "I hereby solemnly swear to never look at you funny again—provided you promise the same. No matter how ridiculous either of us is being. And you promise never to make fun of my dog either."

Dilya hesitated only a moment before hooking her pinky with Linda's and nodding with all the solemnity of a Supreme Court Justice.

"Maybe we should get matching dresses," Dilya firmly declared the topic closed after shaking their joined pinkies up and down three times.

"That wouldn't be very undercover, would it?" Linda did what she could to match the girl's easy tone. "Besides, I don't think we wear quite the same styles." Today Dilya was wearing distressed green jeans that clung tightly to her thin legs, massive black snow boots with all the buckles undone and tinking together with each step like muted sleigh bells, and a heavy red hoodie that asked *Is it too late to be good?* She looked like a dark-haired elf needing only a Santa hat. "You do know that Christmas was *last* month?"

"Duh!"

Right. Because it was a satiric statement about teens never getting their act together. By a teen who apparently had her act *totally* together. Linda knew that was a gift she'd never possessed herself.

"Classy but affordable," Dilya confirmed and led the way.

They walked in silence back along G Street.

"Elegant but will make men's tongues hang out," Dilya said suddenly.

"Dilya!" How old was this girl?

"What my mom—Kee, my adoptive mom, but she cried the

first time I called her Mom and she never cries, so I always give that to her—would call boardroom-street-walker clothes."

"Dilya!" This fifteen-year-old was absolutely not fifteen, except perhaps in her sense of humor. Fine. "Get a grip, kid. What on earth makes you think I could pass as either one, even if I wanted to?"

Dilya stopped right in the middle of the sidewalk and they were nearly plowed under by the hurrying locals. "Hold your hair back in a ponytail and unzip your jacket to here," Dilya pointed to just between Linda's breasts.

She handed Dilya Thor's leash and did as she was ordered, while the girl inspected her critically.

Then Dilya turned to a department store window. Linda hadn't even realized there were department stores here though she'd walked this route every day—except last night of course when she'd been coming from Clive's apartment.

A mannequin in the window wore a fire-engine red sheath dress that clung so tightly that she could see the seam joints in the mannequin itself. It ended about half an inch below the mannequin's crotch. She wore matching red vinyl boots that almost reached the hem, but not quite.

"Not no, but hell no, Dilya."

"Weird," Dilya continued her inspection between Linda and the dummy.

"What?"

"You're right."

"Adults aren't supposed to ever be right?" Linda remembered that clearly from her childhood, but that was because they never were—which didn't bode well at the moment.

"Never, especially not about themselves. Mom acts like she's still working deals on the streets of East LA even when she's busy winning FBI sniper competitions. But you're right. You're super pretty, but you look too nice to be anything bad."

Oh Sweet Christ! The kid was gonna kill her. "Too nice" didn't describe anything that she was or had done since she was younger than Dilya.

"I did say *look* too nice," her smile had a distinctly diabolical twist to it, stating that she'd easily read Linda's expression.

"Dilya, if this is going to work, you're going to have to promise me two things."

"What?"

"One, stop reading my mind."

"No promises."

"Two, don't you dare abandon me in a dress store."

Dilya laughed. "Okay. That part's cool."

They worked their way down the street analyzing the window displays together—each one a different statement: business, sexy, dressy, clubby, and something Dilya called athleisure (designed to make the rich look as if they were also sporty and might actually be willing to get their fingers dirty—if it was for the right activity and didn't muss their hair). When they reached the main entrance, Linda knew one thing for certain: she was even more out of her depth than she'd thought.

CLIVE SCRAPED his third batch of batter into the garbage just as Chef Klaus came over to him. The chocolate kitchen had warmers to melt chocolate, but for baking he had to cross over to the main kitchen.

"What was wrong with that one?"

Not trusting himself to speak in his frustration, Clive handed the chef both a large and a small Pocky stick from his latest test bake.

Klaus took his time inspecting each element. "The shape is good—even and nicely round. You have the color right." He bent each one. Both made a crisp *snap* as he did so. "Good bake."

Then he bit on the small one and grimaced. He picked up the larger one and eyed Clive.

Clive just shook his head. Yes, it was worse. The batter had been fine yesterday. He had no idea what he was doing wrong.

Chef Klaus dropped the sticks on the pile of goo in the garbage can.

"When I become stuck, what I do is go and have a walk."

Clive didn't have time to walk it off. The entire day had been wasted and he—

"Go! *Gehst du hier raus! Spazieren gehen!* Go away! Walk until whatever mess is in your head is cleared out. *Das problem, es ist nicht im* recipe. *Es ist in dem* chef." Then Klaus turned on his heel and walked away.

Clive cleared up his space and hung up his apron. The kitchen was already gearing up for tomorrow night's dinner—a half-dozen chefs scrambling through all of the prep work that could possibly be done in advance. He should be done with the sticks and moving on to the dessert soup. He should have been there hours ago.

Instead, he stepped out of the kitchen and stood in the Basement Hall that connected the kitchen, his shop, flowers, carpentry, and the one-lane bowling alley that ran outward beneath the center of the North Portico's steps.

He couldn't go outside. He might run into Linda walking the fence line with Thor. He absolutely wasn't ready to face that. He didn't know if he'd ever be ready again. His pain and disbelief had turned to the stage of anger and it didn't feel like bargaining was going to happen any time soon. The grief counselor for his mother's death had merely been irritating—anyone tried that on him right now and they might find themselves baked into a cake with four-and-twenty lethal piercings by massive pieces of sugar work.

Walk. Chef Klaus had said to walk and he didn't want to be caught in the back hall ignoring the chef's command. So he walked. When he reached a junction, he turned; when he reached stairs, he descended. When he reached others, he ascended.

All the same to him.

He wasn't going anywhere.

He and Linda weren't— They *definitely* weren't going anywhere. The woman had such a twisted up, demented view of the world that he couldn't imagine what he'd seen in her in the first place.

Sure, she was beautiful. Their bodies had a connection that he'd thought was undeniable. And she had an inner drive that was amazing to witness. So many of the women he met only had an inner drive to power. Linda's was externally focused. She caught bad guys for a living. She—

Why in all creation was he thinking of her? Done. Gone. And the anger inside him flared back to life. The only thing he could equate it to was his father. Clive had hated having a father who showed up for a week every few months and expected no more than his meals and his beer. He gave back even less before departing again—leaving his wife sadder each time. Nic Andrews had sent home his paychecks. He'd only been cruel through emotional negligence, not intention.

Okay, maybe not like Linda.

She'd slashed at him out of—

Clive stumbled to a halt and looked through the doorway in front of him. Miss Watson sat at her dingy desk, her small lamp illuminating only her knitting except for some reflection which lit up her blue eyes. She peered at him in curiosity.

She didn't speak.

At a loss for what else to do, Clive stepped in and sat down on the teetering stool and looked about the tiny, dim office.

"What's with all the books?"

"I'm a librarian."

"A basement librarian?"

She might have smiled. She might not.

"Maybe you're an alien librarian. Is there a tunnel here under the White House that leads to Area 51?"

"That's a long way off," she kept knitting without looking down. He could do that sometimes, when it was a simple pattern and thick yarn. She was doing it on a Fair Isle design, flipping the two yarn colors back and forth with perfect surety.

"Maybe you have a time-space warp under your desk." He wouldn't put it past her. It might explain a few things. "Like in *Star Trek*, you know."

"Yes, I know *Star Trek*."

Clive waited for a while, idly looking at the book titles. Then his eyes traveled up to the only other light in the room. It splashed on the faded and ill-made scarf framed high on the wall.

"It's Belgian," Miss Watson explained without prompting.

"Not a very good job of it."

"It depends on what job you are expecting it to perform."

If there was a double-meaning there somewhere, he couldn't pick it out. "What job *did* it perform? Certainly not keeping out the cold."

"Each five-stitch pairs are five train lines leading into Antwerp that were in view from a particular porch. Two purls were a passenger train, two knits a cargo train, a knit and purl equaled no train. Each group represents ten minutes, each row an hour. The scarf is a chronicle a week long."

"And the dropped stitches?" Clive stood to inspect it more closely.

"Those are the interesting ones. Those are when there was supposed to be a train, but there wasn't."

"Maybe it was running late."

"Actually, it was because the Nazis had replaced it with a war train. You are looking at a coded message of Nazi troop movements in and out of Antwerp prior to the Battle of the Scheldt to wrest it from Nazi occupation in September and October 1944."

Clive could only blink at it in surprise. "Messages in wool."

"Messages in wool," Miss Watson concurred as she continued knitting.

"Anything I should know about those socks you're working on?"

"Yes," then she smiled softly for the first time since he'd met her. It made her seem almost human. "My feet get very cold in January."

The laugh came out of him, breaking so hard in his throat that it hurt. Again and again until he wasn't sure if he was laughing or crying. He clapped a hand over his mouth to stop it before the tiny room was filled with the hysterical sound.

And he could feel the outline of Linda's fine fingers over his mouth on that first visit to his chocolate shop. Her entire face softening as his chocolate made her "have a moment."

That was the woman he had fallen for. But he couldn't reconcile her with the one who had declared there was no such thing as love. If she'd done it in anger, rage, or sorrow, he could have understood. But her voice had been so cold and emotionless that it was impossible to disbelieve her—cold, hard fact. At least for her.

"I'm so sorry, Clive."

Unable to speak, he kept his hand in place over his mouth despite the disconcerting double image of Linda's hand resting there as well.

Miss Watson had put down her knitting and leaned forward into the light so that he could see her face clearly, as if for the first time. She had been, still was, a beautiful woman and the sympathy in her eyes ran deep.

"I should have seen it when I sat with her last night in Lincoln Square. I must be getting old to have missed it. When I teased her about your early arrival at the White House, she didn't react at all. But I missed how cold she went."

He brushed at his eyes before dropping his hand. "She's good at that."

"She'll find her way through it."

He could only shake his head. "No. You didn't see her. You didn't hear what she said." And again his throat tightened too much to allow further speech.

The silence stretched as he fought against the tears—a battle he finally won sometime after Miss Watson's knitting needles began their rhythmic ticking sounds once more.

"I was in love once."

That made him blink in surprise. It was not a possibility he'd ever considered.

"He was a wondrous man and I used our love to betray him for my country. It was the hardest thing I've ever done."

Then she stopped knitting once more and looked at him with those piercing blue eyes. Any hint of softness was gone. Instead, the scary old lady was back and he didn't dare move. He even held his breath.

"It is your job not to give up on her."

"But she—" he could only wave his hand helplessly in the direction of his apartment.

"No!" Miss Watson's voice shifted from dangerous to fierce. "Had I looked deeper, maybe I could have saved him. Had I asked, perhaps he would have come with me. But now I will never know. You must not make that mistake."

"I *did* ask."

"Good! You must not stop doing that."

Clive opened his mouth and closed it again. He didn't know if he dared. Didn't know if he could take the brutal rejection again.

He looked again at the scarf. Not what it appeared to be.

The guns on the walls that barely looked like guns and probably wouldn't at all if taken apart. The crazy collection of books. Not for reading, but for some other, unknowable purpose.

And the woman knitting in the Residence subbasement who was scary, kind, and deeply sad.

None of it what he would expect. None of it quite what it appeared.

He thought of the three Lindas.

The one who gave herself so completely to him...and to her dog. Who hadn't hesitated to help Dilya train Zackie. She gave so easily.

Then there was the intense soldier he'd first witnessed doing her mission at the James J. Rowley Training Center and again in Lafayette Square. Focused, competent...lethal.

And finally the one that he'd only seen once. Getting dressed in front of him as casually as if she was in a locker room. Cold, heartless, frozen to the core. That was the Linda that still made no sense to him. Unless that version wasn't what it appeared to be.

The soldier and the sharing woman were undeniable. The heartless automaton—she was the version of Linda who he couldn't reconcile.

But how to reach past that persona that he'd wager she still wore like armor at this very moment? He knew, he just *knew* that there had to be a way. He couldn't believe that he could fall in love with Linda if her inner essence wasn't the giving woman rather than the automaton.

"She's from Vermont, isn't she?"

"Yes."

He barely heard Miss Watson's reply.

"Vermont," he turned the word over in his mind. Ben and Jerry's Ice Cream. Unlikely flavor combinations. Dairy products, maple syrup, apples, honey.

"She will be attending tomorrow night's reception as a guest," Miss Watson volunteered.

"Really?" Linda at the White House reception in the President's private quarters.

What if he rethought the biscuit dough in his Pocky sticks?
It could—

The concept slammed into him as hard as one of Linda's
kisses.

"Excuse me."

If Miss Watson responded as he hurried out, he didn't hear it.

"YOU'RE TRICKY."

Linda stared down at the pile of dresses on the bench. As
Dilya's taste ran to more covered than revealing, any of them
would have been fine with her. Besides, most of her issues about
showing skin had died during a decade in the Army. She was fine
as long as they didn't go boardroom-street-walker—or whatever
athleisure was—but Dilya was clearly operating to some different
standard.

"No, that bright red doesn't bring out your eyes. Makes you
look kinda demonic."

Demonic fit her current mood well enough at the moment.
Besides…mouse-brown, what color was there to bring out?

"OMG, that makes your hips look as wide as the Hindu Kush."

Linda had patrolled in Afghanistan's Hindu Kush Mountains
and lived to tell the tale—it was the ruggedest and one of the
deadliest areas in the entire war zone. She could do without the
memory—as apparently Dilya also could. That got rid of the
whole peplum theme, which was fine with her. The ruffled flair at
the waist made her feel like a circus clown.

"Nope. Nope. Nope."

"Why not? I thought black dresses were a good thing." Linda
looked at her reflection wearing the clinging jersey material. It
looked good on her. She'd never worn sexy clothes before, but the
startling woman in the mirror wore it well. It clung and curved in
ways that… She sighed. That she'd have liked Clive to have seen

back before she'd destroyed something so good. Why couldn't he have just left things the way they were?

Dilya placed her fists on her hips. "Okay, Miss Undercover Smarty Pants. Sure, it looks majorly awesome on you. Now, where do you put your weapons?"

Linda again turned to the mirror. The cleavage was deep enough to just show where Clive's kiss had healed the wound of her missing dog tags—which now felt like a new scar all its own. But the cleavage was also just deep enough that there was no room to tuck even a Glock Slimline out of sight.

The material flowed over her hips and down to a tasteful overlap that ended mid-thigh. It left her legs bare and the male shop clerk working near the changing rooms seemed to think they were worth a second and a third look.

However, it clung enough that there wasn't anywhere to hide a knife, much less a handgun in a thigh holster or the bulk of a taser. And her draw time from under a dress would be prohibitive.

"What about a jacket of some sort? Then I could wear my usual shoulder holster."

Dilya poked around through the racks and came back with something called a bolero.

"These are so weirdly old-fashioned. I don't know why they make them anymore. It's not like you're a Spanish flamenco dancer or something."

It was the color of the Vermont leaves in autumn, all dark reds and rich golds. Frankly it looked too fancy for her, but Linda shrugged it on anyway, then gasped when she spotted the price tag dangling from the sleeve.

"Hmm," Dilya looked half-pleased, which would be a first in all this madness and which dropped the price from outrageous to incredibly painful. Not that her clothing budget was anything dramatic, but she was presently wearing more than a year's worth of it.

Linda turned to the mirror.

A sexy and sophisticated woman looked back at her. Her mother would approve, which, under the circumstances, Linda supposed was a good thing. The jacket reached down to just below her ribs, emphasizing her reflection's trim waist. It came close enough to closing in the front that she didn't feel quite so revealed, yet stood open enough that it wouldn't inhibit her drawing a weapon. The half-sleeves let the long sleeves of the black dress emphasize her arms.

She shed it, pulled on her shoulder holster, and tugged the jacket back on. A Glock 42 slimline .380 and a lightweight holster would be a better option, but even her big FN Five-seveN was acceptable. Her folding knife and two spare magazines clipped on the other side didn't show at all.

"Not too shabby."

She answered Dilya's "high" praise with an eyeroll that earned her a laugh. If it got her done and out of this store, Linda would find a way to live with the horrific price tag.

She squatted and stood. Twisted side to side testing freedom of movement. She did a quick draw of her weapon, dropping into a crouch with both arms extended and holding the firearm.

And then looked up at the startled faces of three women who had just stepped into the dressing area, their hands full of items on hangars. One of them screamed and sent clothes flying everywhere, which had the clerk rushing over.

"Sorry," Linda reholstered her weapon.

Only Thor's presence with his clearly labeled "Police K-9" harness finally calmed them down. Then they all had to pet and coo over him.

"Can we get out of here?" Linda whispered to Dilya because she didn't know how much more high, squeaky "Oh he's so cute" she could take though Thor was clearly thrilled with the attention.

"Sure. Just as soon as we get a purse you can hide the taser in, then shoes, then deal with your hair."

"You're kidding me, right?" She'd never owned a purse in her life. "No purse. I'll sign out a compact taser and mount it on the harness. I want my hands free."

Dilya's groan of exasperation said that she'd accept that —barely.

"Maybe shoes, maybe." Since all she owned were work boots and running shoes. "But nothing with heels."

Dilya's evil elf smile was back.

Crap!

CHAPTER TWELVE

*C*live was set up for the reception on the Residence's Second Floor in the family kitchen and dining room. Waiters hustled in and out bearing trays of champagne and canapes: bruschetta with smoked salmon and basil, shrimp stuffed with prosciutto and Stilton cheese, and his little chocolate bouquets.

Each bouquet was made up of five slender Pocky sticks thinner than a pencil and half as long. Three shades of chocolate: dark, milk, and white. Then to complement the white, he'd started with a white chocolate base to make two more: blueberry blue and also apple red. He'd made two separate biscuit doughs: a plain one beneath the first four, plus a maple syrup-honey-flavored core for the fifth red stick. All tied so that they stood together like a thistle bloom, using tiny golden ribbons bearing the Vermont state motto: Freedom and Unity.

Chocolate and the American flag—in the flavors and spirit of Vermont.

The guests would all interpret it one way, but he was hoping one person might interpret it another.

He'd worked straight through last night and all day to get these right. For the banquet dessert, he still had the original design: a larger Pocky of plain biscuit and the Vietnamese and Philippine chocolates to complement the soup as well as harkening back to these. But the Pocky bouquet wasn't for the diplomats. The bouquets were designed for one person alone, and never had he worked so hard or felt so inspired to achieve it.

Jacques Torres had always spoken of the dessert of the heart.

Clive had assumed he'd been talking about creating with passion and a desire to discover something new. But now he understood. This treat was so simple and delicate in one way, but in another he had never created anything so perfect. If ever there was to be a single dessert of his heart, this was the one.

He just hoped to god that it worked.

LINDA HAMLIN just hoped to god that she didn't faint.

Unwilling to risk the Secret Service Ready Room close beside the downstairs kitchen, she'd changed into her dress over in the West Wing. Even threats of being tasered hadn't wiped the smiles off any of the agent's faces as she'd stowed her work clothes under a desk in the ready room there.

Captain Baxter waved her into his office as he hung up his phone. He, at least, wasn't leering. Instead he looked grim.

"We just took down a car loaded with weapons. A real mash-up of conventional shit: handguns, shotguns. No sense to it. Not like someone's collection."

"Where?" Linda felt a shiver run up her spine.

"Abandoned on Embassy Row. The guys who dumped it knew where the cameras were well enough to hide their faces."

"Japan's people?"

"Or any of fifty others in that strip. Not quite in anyone's front yard. Your guess is as good as mine. Car rented by a drug runner...who then reported it carjacked."

"What makes you think it was related to us, then?"

"The drug runner was from East LA, never been here before. He received instructions, a plane ticket, and ten grand cash in an unmarked envelope. Did nothing illegal, but I'm holding him for forty-eight hours for 'protection'. He was jacked by, and I'm quoting, 'a couple of Asian dudes with some serious shit.' Chinese Type 77 handguns. He'd never seen them before, but picked them out of a book fast enough. Said having one nearly shoved up his nose had made it real memorable."

"That's a very distinctive weapon, right down to the Chinese star on the handgrip."

"That's what I was thinking. *Too* distinctive. You were right, someone is definitely messing with us tonight. We've got the grounds locked down hard, but you're inside. Keep your eyes open tonight, Hamlin."

Walking across to the Residence had been a major challenge. She'd only partially won the shoe battle with Dilya. She wasn't wearing spikes, but the black ankle boots had a wide two-inch heel that she still didn't have a feel for though she'd practiced with them in her apartment last night. She got lots of practice because it wasn't like she was having any luck sleeping.

Every time she'd lain down, her bed felt cold and empty. And while she lay there studying the ceiling, she'd only been able to remember Clive lying in that Barcalounger like the remains of some innocent, caught in the unexpected blast of an IED. She'd dozed a little. Not enough to dream, but enough for her mind to free associate in a new and hideous fashion. It was as if they had traded places and she was the one lying there with her chest cut open and someone inspecting the empty cavity where her heart should have been.

She'd even tried pulling on her dog tags as she wandered around the tiny apartment—in her new boots—because she couldn't stand being in the bed anymore. All they did was remind her of Clive's kiss that he always had made a point of planting there. She took them off and ended up watching an *I Love Lucy* marathon until it was time to go prepare for the reception.

Linda had spent the entire day at her desk studying the profiles of every guest invited to the reception until she could recite their schooling, family, and career.

And now she was here and couldn't remember how to breathe.

Zackie greeted Thor at the head of the Grand Staircase. Dilya looked elegant, if a little loud, in a bias-cut gold lamé top with a draped collar matched to black slacks. She wore a pretty scarf of green and dark blue, almost big enough to be a shawl.

"I always wear it when I want to be fancy."

"How come I'm stuck in these stupid heels and you get to wear red Converse sneakers?"

"Some of us just have better fashion sense than others." Dilya's smile flashed brilliantly before she and Zackie moved away.

Linda surveyed the layout from the staircase landing at one end of the party. The Center Hall stretched twenty feet wide and over a hundred long including the West Sitting Room through the broad archway beyond. Done in warm beiges and dark wood, it was an attractive space for a party. She almost laughed, a room that would absolutely kill her mother to know that her daughter was invited to. High time that Linda left her grudge behind.

She surveyed the crowd. A pianist played light music at a grand piano tucked close against one wall. There were eight potted palms spaced evenly down the length of the hall with a roughly equal number of Secret Service agents. Small clusters of chairs, some occupied, some not—most people stood. There should be fifty-three guests in all including the three prime ministers and their entourages, scattered in loose groups. Most held wine glasses. A few, she was pleased to see, weren't dressed any fancier than she was. Though she was definitely in the lower-tier amidst so many fine tuxedos and stunning evening gowns, but that didn't matter to her. She was a Secret Service officer here as a guest. As long as she didn't stand out, Dilya had done her job well.

Back at the store, the girl had been oddly shy about Linda's thanks, but accepted the offer of an ice cream sundae readily enough despite the January chill.

Much to her surprise, Linda had some money left over despite the hair and shoes. It was a low trick to play on an unsuspecting dog, but Dilya had leveraged Thor's fame with the store clerk and negotiated such a discount on the dress and jacket that Linda had felt it necessary to tip him generously when Dilya wasn't watching. Or when she thought Dilya hadn't been—the way she'd played with Thor afterward said that the girl had been crafty and calculated the entire deal. A child raised in a barter-based society clearly enjoyed outsmarting a retail-based one. And she'd seen it far enough ahead to tell Linda that she had to bring Thor to go dress shopping.

As she stepped into the hall, Linda almost lost her balance when her heel caught the edge of the carpet.

Thor glanced up at her.

"Watch it or I'll put you in heels and see how you do."

Thor looked unperturbed.

Linda began matching up faces and names. The First and Second Couples were easy. Former President Matthews was also in attendance—his wife's plane had been delayed and she wouldn't be here until tomorrow's meetings. She had no official capacity, but had close relations with all three guest countries through her UNESCO work.

The leaders of the three guest countries were chatting with their American counterparts. There hadn't been anything damning in any of their files.

She spotted Harvey Lieber standing in a shadow along one of the walls, but close by the President. He afforded her a brief nod before turning back to study the room. The President shifted down the hall to join another conversation and Lieber followed. A massive black man did the same for former President Matthews.

Speaker of the House. Majority and minority whips of the

Senate. Secretary of Defense Archie Stevenson—a tall and spare man with light brown hair—was having a heated debate with Secretary of State Mallinson. Despite Archie's attempts to remain calm, Mallinson was waving his hands about in such a way that a nearby Secret Service agent shuffled farther along the wall to avoid being impaled.

Not a hard choice on who to root for—Secretary Stevenson was Dilya's adoptive father, which was recommendation enough for Linda. Not wanting to enter Mallinson's sphere of intolerable officiousness, she decided to circle the other way.

Thor had already proven that he didn't need to be "on task" to find explosives—three days ago they'd just been walking to work when he'd detected the diplomat—she simply let him choose her way into the room but kept his leash short. She had tried to groom him for the event. However, his crazy tangle of fur that seemed to grow in every direction, but mostly straight out, looked much the same before and after brushing. She hoped her own hair wasn't too much the same.

Thor drifted over to Agent Lieber, sniffed, then wagged up at him in greeting.

"Go away, you." Linda couldn't tell if he was addressing Thor or herself. "Do your damn job." Okay, that one she got, and signaled Thor to keep moving. They moved slowly up the south side of the hall until they reached the grand double-arched window that seemed to be in every movie ever made about the White House. That she was suddenly standing in the real-life version of the movie set made her wish once again that she was just out walking the fence line and had never heard of Miss Watson or the White House Protection Force.

Taking a deep breath for fortitude, which didn't provide any help at all, she crossed to the north side and began working her way back along the hall.

She made it about twenty feet before she plowed squarely into Clive's back.

CLIVE HAD JUST WANTED to take a peek into the West Sitting Hall to see how his part of the appetizer was faring. None were coming back on the serving trays, which he took as a good sign, but neither was much of anything else. He wanted to know if his were being eaten first or last of the selection.

At least that's what he told himself he was doing. He'd just step out, take a quick look, and then duck back into the dining room to continue the service.

He wouldn't be searching up the hall to see if there was a flounce of shining cocoa hair anywhere among the crowd. He wasn't going to stoop that low.

Clive stepped into the hall and someone slammed into his back.

He tried to take a stumbling step forward, but a small dog—Thor—had circled around from behind him and stood with his forepaws practically on Clive's shoes, happily wagging his tail. Unable to step forward, and overbalanced from behind, he went down like a drunkard on a storm-tossed sea. No handy furniture near enough to catch himself with, he crashed down on the rug. His tall chef's hat tumbled away. Thor immediately raced over and stuck his head inside it.

Well, at least Clive knew who had hit him.

As did everyone else in the entire hall—they were all looking in his direction. As payback for bowling her into the men's lavatory in the West Wing in front of her boss, this struck him as somewhat over the top.

Thor tried to lift his head, but in the process, the chef's hat slid down to his neck. He began shaking his head trying to free himself as the crowd began laughing.

He lay there for a moment, focused on just how amazing two-inch heels made Linda's legs look. The muscles in her calves were accentuated wonderfully, especially as he knew exactly how they felt when wrapped around— The past. Again!

She helped him back to his feet with a strength that was now very familiar. Except it was attached to a woman he barely recognized. Once he was stable, she moved forward and plucked his hat off Thor's head and handed it back to him.

At the crowd's applause, Thor wagged his tail.

The only thing that Clive could think to do was bow and then retreat back into the dining room. He was not, however, so addled that he failed to drag Linda along with him.

"I'm so sorry. Are you okay?"

He looked down at her and couldn't speak.

Linda Hamlin in a dress. He'd never thought to imagine such a thing. The black dress clung to her and told him just how lucky he was…had been…to have a lover with a body like that. The jacket accentuated the color of her hair and brought out a slightest hint of deep red in the brown that he'd never noticed before. Her casually ragged cut had been transformed to accentuate all of her features and Linda was a woman with many, many fine features: bright eyes, wide mouth, pert nose…

"You changed your hair." Which was perhaps the dumbest phrase ever uttered by man.

"And I'm wearing a dress," her voice laced with deep chagrin and just a bit of the humor that he'd forgotten how much he missed.

"I noticed. My god, Linda. I can't begin to tell you…" *how much I've missed you* "…how incredible you look."

She grimaced, then scowled at somewhere near the center of his chest.

Just as she opened her mouth, the head of the PPD strode into the dining room.

"Hamlin. We aren't paying you to chat up the chefs. Now get a move on."

And without another word, he strode back out.

"What was…"

"Senior Special Agent Harvey Lieber hates me," Linda patted his arm. "But he's right. The trouble in Lafayette Square isn't over. I think it's hitting the fan tonight. Here at the reception if I'm right."

"Have you…" No, of course, she hadn't tasted one of his appetizers. She was in her focused-soldier mode. He swiveled to a passing tray and snatched a salmon bruschetta and handed it to Thor, who scarfed it down in a single bite. That delayed Linda just long enough for him to place a Pocky stick bouquet in her hand. "Try this. Please."

Then, though it nearly killed him to do so, he turned her around and pushed lightly against her shoulders to send her back into danger. Because that was a part of who she was and it wasn't up to him to keep her close and safe—no matter how much he wanted to.

COURTESY OF HER STUPID HEELS, Linda practically did a Clive-style pratfall at his light push. It was either that or her weak knees. Whichever it was, she managed to keep on her feet by only the narrowest of margins. Even standing before him for just those few moments had stirred up things she didn't understand until she was nearly swept under by vertigo.

But few heads turned as she stumbled out into the long hall once more.

East. She'd been moving east along the north side of the hall when she'd run into Clive.

So she continued east and let Thor lead the way. She was a professional and could guide him, but she didn't feel up to leading at the moment. Only as she passed a small group of senators talking with Vice President Daniel Darlington did she remember to look at what Clive had given her. A tiny bouquet of multicolored Pocky sticks in the colors of chocolate and the American flag wrapped in the golden ribbon bearing the Vermont state motto: "Freedom and Unity."

She nibbled on one while she focused on getting her mind out of the kitchen and back into the hall. The chocolate was so good, even sublime compared to the samples he'd given her a lifetime ago in his chocolate shop.

A senior aide, who she couldn't place at the moment—the head speechwriter?—stopped her to thank her and Thor for the fine work in Lafayette Square.

The blueberry one took her back to her childhood in Vermont —back before she'd understood that her family was a nightmare. There'd been a big blueberry bush in the backyard—might even still be there—and she remembered every summer, standing out in the sunshine, picking and filling her mouth as fast as she could. The little blue Pocky burst with the flavor of nostalgia so richly that she wondered if the speechwriter thought that it was his thanks that prompted her misty eyes.

She was halfway back to her original starting point when she ate the final red one. It wasn't strawberry as she'd expected. Instead it was an explosion of Macintosh apple. Vermont in the fall slammed into her senses. Then she crunched down on the biscuit center and the flavor of maple syrup washed over her like the cusp of winter-to-spring when the maple tree sap was flowing but there was still snow on the ground.

Clive had made a treat of the seasons of Vermont.

She looked around and saw that they were the first items being swept off the trays that the waiters were carrying guest-to-guest. It seemed that everyone was holding the little golden ribbons. He'd made a treat for the reception that was the clear favorite.

That wasn't right. Yes, it was a clear favorite, but how many people would understand that it was the seasons of Vermont? And Clive had said he was from San Francisco and had worked in LA, New York, Virginia... He'd never once mentioned Vermont.

She'd said nothing beyond the fact that she'd grown up there.

From that single clue, Clive had developed this magnificent treat for her alone. She had said such awful, unforgivable things to him, and he had given her back the best parts of her childhood. He'd fed a treat to the elite of Washington, DC, that was designed just for her.

"Are you okay?"

She could only shake her head and she focused on the man who had come up to her. Tall, lean, a tousle of light brown hair—Secretary of Defense Archibald Stevenson III and former major of the 160th Night Stalkers.

"You're Dilya's father."

That earned her a surprisingly cheery, lopsided smile. "You've met her?"

"She helped me buy this dress. Jacket. Shoes." Could she sound any more like a driveling idiot? "Told the salon how to do my hair." Yes, apparently she could. Because her hair was *exactly* the sort of thing that the Secretary of Defense would care about.

"Allow me to say that she did a damn nice job. And that would make you Sergeant Hamlin and Thor. I was briefed on the work you did. Thank you for that."

She considered alerting him that it wasn't over yet, but the head of the Presidential Protection Detail had deemed it need-to-know only, so she kept her mouth shut.

"What happened to your friend?" Not her smoothest subject change.

"Friend?"

"You were, uh," she'd dug the hole and couldn't figure a way out of it. Fine. Might as well dig it deeper. "What did you do with Secretary of State Mallinson's body?"

"Excuse me?" He didn't sound offended, merely surprised.

"You weren't exactly seeing eye-to-eye earlier. You're the man left standing, so I figure you won or you did him in. Should I start checking behind the potted palms?"

His smile was more of a grimace.

"He has always been stubborn man, but tonight he was being stupid to the point of irrationality. It was as if none of his thoughts were connecting. Made me positively twitchy."

"I'll definitely start checking behind the palms."

"Don't bother. He just left. Said he had a meeting to get to."

"Oh, well. It was a pleasure to meet you, sir." The prime minister of Vietnam came their way and she decided it was best if she bowed out.

She checked her watch—the pretty feminine one that Dilya had insisted that she buy to replace her favorite Luminox Blackout military one. At least she'd been able to read that one. She squinted for fashion. Never again.

Twenty-six more minutes to the reception. Then down to the East Room for the dinner. She had been so sure that whatever was planned was going to happen at this reception, but nothing looked out of place.

———

THEY WERE NEARING the end of service for the reception. Clive was arranging the last of his Pocky treats. Next up would be to race down the narrow spiral stairs that connected the kitchens: the Second Floor kitchen, the pantry close by the State Dining Room, the main kitchen on the Ground Floor, subbasement storage, and finally the second subbasement dishwashing room. The sous chefs should have the white chocolate-pomegranate *baba ghanoush* of the first course ready, but he wanted to check each plate himself while the diners were finding their seats.

Seeing Linda had given him such hope. Miss Watson had been right. He shouldn't give up, no matter what. One look at her and he'd known. Okay, two. The first look had been him trying to comprehend what a stunningly gorgeous woman it had been his good fortune to find. But with the second look he'd seen the pain clear in her eyes. He *knew* for an absolute fact—as surely as dark chocolate and strawberries were a perfect match—that the real woman inside Linda-the-soldier was the one with the giving heart, not the automaton.

He wanted to see her again, right now.

But, she'd said there was danger here at the reception and that meant she was working. Special Agent Harvey Lieber's furious reminder must mean that the danger was imminent and somehow Linda and Thor were the key to finding it.

Hadn't Miss Watson said something about Linda being added to the guest list?

To the *guest* list. Not the *agent* list.

That meant that she wasn't here as an agent, yet the head of the Presidential Protection Detail had made it clear that she was. And if she'd merely been a guest, she probably wouldn't have brought Thor.

Linda with Thor.

That's what was going on out there while he was in here making chocolate doodads. He looked down at the last tray of Pocky stick bouquets and felt more useless than ever before in his life. More useless than a young boy unable to attract his father's attention. More useless than holding his mother's hand as she died and unable to do anything to stop the process.

But there'd been a moment when he'd done something important. Maybe even more important than chocolate. Just a few days ago in Lafayette Square, he'd somehow managed to help Linda. A path that had led her here tonight.

Well, he couldn't help her from here in the dining room. And he'd be of even less use from the downstairs kitchen.

He returned to finishing up the last tray. This one he would carry out into the hall personally. If there was any way that he could help Linda, he wasn't going to cower in the kitchen just because it was dangerous.

OUT OF IDEAS, Linda had sought out Dilya.

She had nothing but a hunch that anything was going to happen tonight and she now doubted every assumption that had led her here.

But she'd still be happier if she could at least send Dilya out of harm's way, even if she couldn't justify clearing the room. The threat wasn't credible. A block of C-4 in a diplomatic pouch didn't mean anything. That had been outside the security bubble that enclosed the White House. It was nearly impossible to bring anything lethal through that barrier.

She found the teen near the center of the hall. It was only after she stepped into the conversation that she really focused on the man Dilya was talking to.

Former President Peter Matthews.

He was tall, handsome, and graying at the temples. He looked ten times as impressive in real life as he did on television.

Dilya still had Zackie beside her and she was arguing with the former President. "She is *not* hopeless. Her only problem is that she hasn't been trained to be more than a pet."

"And you're going to make a military dog out of Anne's Sheltie?"

"Sure," Dilya told him blithely. "And Linda promised to help me," Dilya turned to her.

She had? Well, to escape the dress store and then the shoe store and then the salon, she may have made any number of promises. "I'm glad to."

"But that dog has a brain the size of a peanut." As if to prove his point, the President tossed a stuffed shrimp on the floor in front of Zackie, who barked at it rather than eating it. "I win."

Dilya sighed. "Thor's smart though, isn't he?"

"At least around food." Linda snapped her fingers, then pointed at the shrimp. Thor—who'd been sitting patiently beside her—lunged in, snapped up the shrimp, and returned to his position to eat it happily.

"*He's* well behaved," the President bent down to pet him.

"Trained at a ranch in Montana."

"Henderson's," he acknowledged. Then he froze, half bent over, before straightening slowly.

At first she was shocked that he knew the origin of her dog. But that didn't explain why he was startled to be caught with that knowledge.

The only reason that she could think of for him to be surprised was if Henderson's Ranch was more than it seemed. What if it was...

"WHPF," Linda said to him.

"What's that?" But his poker face sucked. Even she could read it.

"White House Protection Force, sir."

Captain Baxter had said that the former President had certified the WHPF personally. Somehow, her dog and the WHPF were linked to one another.

He sighed, then shrugged his complicity.

Now it was Dilya's turn to say, "What's that? What's WHPF? And what does Major Beale's ranch have to do with it?"

"Hush, half pint," the former President looked down at her. "Keep your mouth shut on this one. Not even your parents."

Dilya nodded, but it was clear that she wasn't going anywhere.

The former President sighed again. "Always have to have your nose in it, don't you, Dilya?"

"Survival instinct," Dilya answered flatly and Linda knew that it was true, even though it made Dilya blush to be caught telling a real truth.

"I wish I could have done more," President Matthews sighed,

apparently missing the depth of Dilya's statement. "Not a lot of things for an ex-President to do. I'm not exactly the kind of guy who sits around in some consulting think tank. The WHPF has a good purpose behind it. I liked it and Emily agreed to set it up for me."

Emily Beale. Major Emily Beale, formerly of the Night Stalkers. Linda had met her once, sort of. The Night Stalkers 5th Battalion D Company had transported her Ranger unit into a strike zone five years ago. There was no question that the reason they'd escaped the horrendous battle so unscathed had been largely due to the pilot of the team's DAP Hawk, one Major Emily Beale—rumored to be the best pilot they'd ever had.

Now she'd created the White House Protection Force, which had earned Baxter's and Lieber's absolute respect. And the WHPF had been the one to make sure Linda was assigned to this duty—undercover protection of the President, who was presently standing not twenty feet behind the former President.

"*Be all your dog can be.*" The flyer in her DD 214 discharge packet had somehow come from Henderson's Ranch.

"Emily's dog trainer uses that phrase all the time," the President explained. "Ex-SEAL, quite a character."

A SEAL dog trainer at a ranch run by the Night Stalkers' best pilot who had set up the White House Protection Force and then managed to get Linda assigned right into the center of it.

No pressure.

Of course Linda was a former sergeant of the 75th Rangers. Pressure was what she ate for lunch.

She scanned the room again. These were hers to protect, but she didn't know how. The Secretary of Defense was now talking to a short, very buxom woman with a blonde streak in her Asian dark hair. The woman stood as Dilya might indeed describe a boardroom-street-walker—she looked sharp, classy, and just maybe a bit on the hustle. And quite pregnant. When she went up on tiptoes to kiss the Secretary, that confirmed her as Dilya's adoptive mother.

There was no way Linda could get them out of the room without raising the alarm. And Linda wasn't going to allow Dilya to lose another set of parents. She'd been orphaned at eleven, the same age Linda herself might as well have been. The girl had been fortunate enough to find new parents, a gift beyond any measure.

She had to solve this.

The contrast of Dilya's mom beside Secretary Stevenson versus Secretary of State Mallinson was startling. One content to stand quietly while her husband rested a testing hand on her mounded abdomen—the other near to raving.

But Mallinson had left for a meeting.

A meeting.

Lieutenant Jurgen had used exactly that same excuse to get away from her after she'd nailed his training course—back then she had trusted the instructor to not be the agent of destruction. An oversight that still made her grind her teeth whenever she remembered it.

But no one set up a meeting during a State Dinner. And then to attend only half of the reception? What had Mallinson been trying to get away from?

The itch between her shoulder blades bloomed to life.

"Excuse me," she walked away from the former President in midsentence of teasing Dilya and strode over to Harvey Lieber, lurking in his shadow. "If he's still here, don't let Secretary of State Mallinson off the property."

"What?"

"Do it! Then have them check him for a trigger of some sort."

To his credit, whatever he thought of her, Lieber didn't hesitate to raise his wrist mic and send out the instruction.

His eyes unfocused as he listened.

"Nothing. Nothing," he echoed the reports for her. "Got him. Treasury Building tunnel—unusual exit for him. Pissed as hell.

Making a lot of threats." His eyes refocused on her. "No trigger on him. Not even a cell phone. You sure about this, Hamlin?"

"Pissed or scared?"

He relayed the question and merely looked thoughtful at the reply.

"Get him back here," she looked around the room. They couldn't bring him to the Second Floor without creating a panic. She quickly reviewed the map in her head. Most of the Ground Floor would be filled with guests who even at this moment were gathering for the main party to descend the Grand Staircase and lead them to dinner. Except for…

"Take him to the Usher's Room by the North Entrance."

She didn't bother to wait. Instead, she crossed the hall—as casually as she could manage, which only got her stopped twice for congratulations and Thor petted three times—then raced down the back stairs toward the State Floor.

Clive was still somewhere in the upstairs hall. If she was wrong, or too slow, he could well be in harm's way. She moved faster, despite her unfamiliar heels.

CHAPTER THIRTEEN

Clive made sure his chef's hat was on straight, then swept
up the last finished tray of treats and carried them out
into the reception himself.

Only after he stepped out did he double-check that Linda
wasn't about to barrel into him or trip him up again. No sign of
her and no Thor.

He turned for the main body of the room.

Everyone went out of their way to take another Pocky treat off
the tray as he worked his way forward. The compliments flew
thick and fast but he barely heard them, though he made sure to
nod and smile as seemed appropriate.

The First Lady made a point of stopping him and
complimenting him on the success. "They swept every tray clean
before they touched anything else," she told him. "Of course, it *was*
chocolate, so I was an easy sell and have eaten entirely too many."

He exchanged a laugh with her.

Linda, however, was anything but an easy sell—even with
chocolate. Had she tried the treat? Had she understood?

He'd put everything he had into it.

And now?

He used his height to scan the crowd once more.

And now she was nowhere to be seen.

LINDA ALMOST RACED past the Office of the Chief Usher. It was on the landing between the two flights of the back stairs leading from the Second Floor of the Residence to the double-high main Entrance Hall. At the bottom of the stairs was the Usher's Room, but Thor had veered aside at this midlevel office and she saw why.

Handler Jim and his springer spaniel Malcolm were standing just inside the threshold of the Office of the Chief Usher. A number of people were packed into the small room.

"Thought it best to bring him in here," he greeted her. "Get him away from the State Floor and the main entrance. Folks are pouring in at the moment."

"Perfect," she briefly squeezed his arm in thanks as she stepped past him.

The office was on the mezzanine level—directly above the Ushers' Room and only accessible by these back stairs. At most it measured ten by fifteen feet, though it felt much smaller with Malcolm, four agents, the chief usher, and Secretary Mallinson all squeezed in around the pristine walnut desk and chairs.

Malcolm hadn't alerted to Secretary Mallinson. Neither had Thor and he still wasn't. No explosives on him. Nor had he recently handled any.

Linda's thoughts raced, just like when she and her dog were at point on a village patrol.

"I don't suppose you're willing to be helpful?"

Mallinson leaned back against the wall with his arms crossed over his chest and a worried look on his face. He glanced up at the ceiling at her question, then looked sharply away as if he'd been caught with his hand in the cookie jar.

No longer any doubt that she'd found her culprit.

But he wasn't showing any fear. Whatever he'd planted up there, he was convinced that he was safe down here.

However, his nerves were high. He checked his watch twice in under ten seconds before he caught himself.

"I don't know what you're talking about. I have a crucial meeting." He protested vehemently, but his eyes drifted to the ceiling once more.

She turned to Jim. "Is Malcolm trained in tracing lost articles?"

He shook his head, "Just explosives."

That wasn't going to help. She and Thor had checked the entire hall and found nothing.

Linda looked down at her dog. "Time to see just how good your training was, little one."

She pointed at the Secretary and said, "Thor, *verloren.*" Lost.

He sniffed the man carefully, then looked back up at her.

The Secretary stared down at him in shock. He began protesting loudly, but she ignored the distraction.

Hoping for the best, Linda pointed out the door toward the stairs leading up to the reception.

"*Such!*" Seek!

SEARCHING AMONG THE GUESTS, Clive had at least spotted Dilya. If anyone knew where Linda had gone, it would be the kid.

He was a little daunted by the company she was keeping, but took a deep breath and braved it anyway. In Lafayette Square, he'd stepped into danger without knowing it. That wasn't bravery. This time, he knew that whatever was going to happen, he was probably now standing near the center.

"Good Evening, Mr. President."

"Chef Andrews," President Matthews sounded delighted. "You were always one of my wife's favorites."

"And she mine as well, sir. She was kind enough to bring me

chocolate from her family's own plantation on several occasions. She has very much made me want to visit Vietnam."

"If you bring some of your finished chocolate back with you, I can't imagine you won't be welcome. This," he picked one of the last treats up from Clive's tray, "is utterly delightful."

"Thank you, sir."

Dilya, however, appeared to be too distracted to take another. That was very unusual, especially because he suspected that she was one of the chief thieves of his shop's small chocolate cabinet.

She kept watching an archway off the side of the hall. It led to one of the bedrooms, or maybe the family elevator, which he'd never used.

He was about to scan the room again when Linda and Thor appeared beneath the arch as if by magic. Or as if she'd been running, and had suddenly come to a halt and was trying to appear calm.

Then Linda softly snapped her fingers and, when Thor looked up at her, she pointed to the left.

Thor put his head down and went.

He recognized the action from the very first moment he'd seen her at the starting line of the James J. Rowley Training Center's explosives course. With gestures and small noises, she guided him forward.

Very few people were watching. Dilya. Lieber and Adams from the Secret Service agents along the wall. But no one else. Not even President Matthews, who had turned to strike up a conversation with his replacement, President Zachary Thomas—something about rival football teams.

The conversations still buzzed up and down the length of the room. The pianist still played though Clive doubted anyone was listening to him to begin with.

He and Dilya watched as Thor suddenly shifted direction, then sat abruptly at someone's feet.

"Oh shit!" Dilya whispered softly.

Clive didn't bother to correct her language. He just put an arm around her shoulder and pulled her in tight as Secretary of Defense Archibald Stevenson looked down at Thor in surprise.

"GOOD EVENING, SIR," Linda managed as the shock rippled through her.

"Good evening again, Ms. Hamlin. May I ask why your dog is looking at me like that?" Both of Dilya's parents would know the meaning of the way Thor had sat so abruptly.

This couldn't be happening. She *couldn't* be the one to take away Dilya's second set of parents.

Then Thor stretched up to sniff at the Secretary's hand.

"I'm sorry to ask this, sir, but did you shake hands with Secretary of State Mallinson?"

He lifted his right hand up to near his face, inspecting it and then Thor.

Then he held it down closer to Thor—who wriggled happily in response at finding what he'd been told to find.

"I did. What is going on, Ms. Hamlin?"

"I'm sorry, but I don't have time to explain."

"Yes, I think you do," Dilya's mom stepped directly in front of her.

"No, ma'am. I really don't." Then she looked down at Thor. "*Such!*" And they stepped around the couple and continued down the room.

"OH MY GOD, I thought I was gonna die," Dilya bolted from Clive's grasp and raced to her parents, where she hugged them fiercely. They pulled her in close.

That was real family. That's what Clive had lost with the death of his mother. Lost and missed so much that he'd thought it was a hole that could never be filled. Until he met Linda Hamlin.

He couldn't take his eyes from the three of them holding on so tightly to everything they had, but they in turn never took their eyes off Linda and her dog as the team continued their patrol.

He and Linda and a girl of their own.

It was all he needed to be happy—a truth he no longer doubted in the slightest.

Clive could feel the seconds ticking by, so slowly that each heartbeat seemed to be a separate clap of thunder in his ears.

Linda came up to him in full soldier mode.

Thor sniffed him, then moved on. Even the dog was in soldier mode and acted as if he didn't recognize Clive.

Then, just before Thor led her away, Linda reached out to squeeze his hand.

"That chocolate was truly glorious, Clive. Thank you."

And she was gone.

But she'd left hope in her wake.

LINDA COULD FEEL the clock ticking. Inevitable. Unstoppable. How many seconds did she have? Not enough was her fear. Though at least she now knew Thor could track an odor.

But she'd taken a precious few of those seconds to try and tell Clive what he'd done to her. His chocolate treat had gifted her back so much of the past she had forgotten. She and Peggy, back when they were still friends, on the swing hanging from the old apple tree. Maple sugar eaten fresh off the snow where Old Man Kimball would drizzle it in fanciful swirls to cool. All of the tastes and flavors of her childhood, distilled down to the impossible essence of five little sticks of chocolate.

How had he reached so deep inside himself that he could do that?

He was the one who had given her that gift. And she knew he hadn't had the snack figured out yet on that awful night when she'd gone out of her way to wound him.

Instead of anger or revenge, he had reached out to her with impossible forgiveness that she didn't deserve. Forgiveness and understanding.

If he truly gave her another chance, she promised herself that she would never again cast it aside.

Of course, he wasn't the only one who had to give them another chance. She first had to make sure they all survived.

President. Vice President. Prime ministers. Some noticed Thor's inspection, but most continued their discussions, oblivious to what was going on around them.

Until Thor once again sat abruptly.

She looked up at the man's eyes.

"The one you least suspect," she whispered.

Special Agent Harvey Lieber glared back at her.

CLIVE MOVED IN FAST, using his bulk to block any escape, as well as anyone else's view.

"Not me," the agent growled.

Clive looked down and saw that Linda had a small taser pressed against the belly of the head of Presidential Protection Detail, Harvey Lieber.

"Are you sure, Linda?" Clive couldn't believe it.

"Shut up, Clive. This is out of your league."

"And yours, Hamlin," Lieber growled at her.

Clive couldn't believe it—the head of the PPD? He glanced around, but they still had no one else's attention, not even of the other agents in the hall. Only the trio of Dilya's family watched them from the far side of the hall.

"We can walk out of here quietly, Lieber. Or I can have you dragged out of here twitching like a string puppet."

"Not gonna happen, Hamlin. You and your dog screwed up. You're both gone."

Clive glanced down at Thor, who was still sitting close by Agent Lieber's feet. But he wasn't looking up at the agent the way that he'd been looking up at the Secretary's hand. Instead, he was staring down.

"Linda?"

"Clive, I said—"

"Look at Thor."

Linda and Lieber both turned to face him, then they both looked down at the dog.

Lieber took a slow, cautious step sideways, but Thor's attention didn't follow.

For the moment, Agent Lieber had been standing in the shadow of one of the potted palms.

A briefcase sat behind the pot.

"Oh shit," Linda muttered. She'd been hunting the scent of explosives before, not of Secretary Mallinson. "I knew I should have checked behind the palms."

"It's the same make and model," Linda was going to be sick.

"You sure?" Lieber asked.

"I spent half an hour staring at it in the middle of Lafayette Square and then another dozen looking at the photos in the debriefing. I have nightmares about this make of briefcase."

"I'll call the bomb squad. I had already alerted them and they're staging in the basement." She caught his wrist and kept him from raising his mic.

"It may not be fast enough." She tried to check her pretty ladies' watch, but there'd been no outer dial to spin and track the number of remaining minutes. And she couldn't remember now.

She squinted at it.

Five minutes to go until it was time to head downstairs?

No, three. Could the bomb squad even get here that fast?

Would it be safe to move? A motion trigger or—

"Secretary Mallinson kept checking his watch. That implies a timer, not a motion detector." Linda reached for the case and this time Lieber stopped her.

"What if it's both?"

She closed her eyes and tried to picture Mallinson's face. He'd checked his watch, not once but multiple times. He wasn't worried about her moving it. He was worried about her finding it too soon.

Brushing Lieber aside, she picked up the case.

She lived through it.

Good sign!

"This way," Clive stepped out ahead of her, and she followed closely in the wake he cut through the crowd with his empty tray leading the way.

All she could think about was that, moments ago, her hand had clutched his, perhaps for the last time. And now it was holding a briefcase that felt as if it was leaving a stain of evil that would never wash off.

By the time she noticed where he was leading her, they were past the back stairs. Past the stairs, through the dining room, and into the First Family's private kitchen.

"What?"

"Here," Clive slammed open the dumbwaiter.

No time to stop and think, she shoved it in among the dirty serving platters.

Clive slammed the door shut and hit the button for the downstairs kitchen.

Lieber called down to the bomb squad.

The three of them stood still. Unable to move away despite how stupidly close they were to the dumbwaiter filled with explosives. If the bomb went off in the shaft, it was bound to shoot a column of flame straight up at them. Still they all crowded around the glass doors and looked down.

"At the kitchen level," Lieber reported as he listened to his earpiece.

"Bomb squad has it… In a portable shock sleeve…" which would absorb at least some of the explosion. "Out of the building…"

Then a pause long enough that Linda almost screamed for them to hurry.

"Inside containment with vessel sealed…"

"Detonated! No damage. No one hurt."

And all three of them whooshed out held breaths making them laugh nervously together.

LIEBER DIDN'T SAY A WORD. He simply shook Clive's hand, a solid grip that expressed all of his relief at a close call. He held Linda's hand in both of his for a long moment as they exchanged silent nods. Then he knelt down in front of Thor and received a sharp growl for his efforts.

"*Gute Hund. Freund.*"

Thor relaxed at her command and accepted the pet, but still showed the man distrust.

Lieber rose and headed toward the hall calling instructions into his wrist mic to prepare for the processional to dinner.

Unsure what to do with his hands, Clive wiped them on his apron, then threaded his fingers together.

Linda looked up at him, inspecting him closely.

"What?"

"You're a brave man, Clive Andrews."

"You think that's brave? You should try building a three-hundred-pound chocolate White House that's going to appear on national television at Christmas. That's bravery." Then he blew out another breath at how ridiculous he sounded.

She rested her hand over his interlaced fingers. He could feel the gentle impression of each of her fingers as they held his.

"You are also the kindest man I've ever met. I can't believe that you made that chocolate treat for me after what I did to you."

"It was all for you, Linda." And if he was going to be brave... "I love you, Linda Hamlin. I know it's too soon. I know it's ridiculous. But I could never ask for more than you. I get that it may take you some time to catch up, but Miss Watson said to never stop saying it."

"Miss Watson, huh?" A ghost of a smile touched her lovely lips.

"Scary lady in the dingy basement? You know."

"Yes, I know Miss Watson. At least a little," her expression was confused for a moment, but she shrugged it away.

Clive couldn't think of what else to say.

Then the kitchen phone rang, the display showing Chef Klaus' extension. He freed one hand from Linda's grasp but made sure to keep a hold with the other so that she couldn't slip away, then pressed the speaker button.

"Andrews here."

"*Warum* are you up there? *Du musst hierher kommen.* While you are playing with your chocolates upstairs, *wir haben* bomb squads who say nothing, secret service agents who *auch nichts sagen.* All is mayhem. We start service *in neun minuten.* Get down here. *Schnell! Schnell!*" He delivered the tirade in a single breath intermixed with a thick stream of German curses, then the line went dead.

"I guess I'd better get going," Clive could stand here all night holding Linda's hand in his. He squeezed her fingers and she squeezed them back.

"I don't have the words, Clive."

He did his best not to show his disappointment.

"But," she took a deep breath and let it out slowly, "but if you can give me some time, I promise to try to find them."

Without thinking, he gathered her into his arms and held tight. And she held him back.

For now that was enough.

The phone rang again. They both looked at the display declaring it was again from Chef Klaus.

Clive didn't bother to answer it. Instead, he kissed Linda far too briefly, then raced down the tight spiral staircase that descended close beside the dumbwaiter.

LINDA FELT a little dazed and lightheaded as she stepped out into the hall. It was completely transformed.

The crowds were all gone, as was the pianist. A waiter picked up dishes and glasses and a janitor followed closely behind cleaning every cleared surface. A large vacuum cleaner started up at the far end of the hall.

Only five people remained: Dilya with her parents, former President Matthews, and a huge black man who must be his bodyguard.

Dilya rushed over, slamming into her arms and giving her such a hard hug that it took her breath away. Linda hugged her back and took the brief liberty of resting her cheek on the girl's hair. Her parents were so lucky. Though it wasn't all luck. They were parents who behaved the way parents were supposed to.

"It appears that you had an interesting evening," President Matthews commented drily.

Then Kee Stevenson, Dilya's mom, stepped over, planting her feet firmly on the carpet and her fists on her hips. She looked as if she could whip Linda's ass one-handed, despite being pregnant.

"Did you just nearly get our daughter killed?"

Linda could only nod. If she'd been even two minutes slower, they'd all be dead. She squeezed Dilya once more and let her go before the teen could figure out she'd actually bonded with an adult.

"Damn it!" Kee pounded a heel on the carpet. "God damn you, Archie."

Linda could only blink in surprise. She'd thought she was the one in trouble.

"You know how much I hate being out of the action. You ever try your 'wouldn't it be fun to have another kid' pitch on me again, I'm gonna bust your balls."

"Better than my arm," Secretary Stevenson, proving he was a brave man, simply stepped in and slid an arm around his wife's shoulder.

Kee slammed an elbow into his gut, but he was braced for it and merely laughed.

"That was really cool, Thor," Dilya squatted down to play with him.

"Ma'am," the massive agent came up beside them. He tapped his earpiece. "I've been asked to pass on to you that initial analysis shows that the explosive was TMETN."

"Odorless. That would explain why the dogs didn't alert to it. But the power..." The briefcase hadn't been very heavy. Linda didn't see how that little weight would do more than kill the few people closest to it.

"TMETN and sarin gas. Probably in containers shaped to look like normal objects when X-rayed. If the agents X-rayed the Secretary of State's briefcase at all," the last was delivered with a snarl that said on his watch it damn well would have been.

There was a stunned silence. Everyone on the entire Second Floor of the Residence would have been dead within ten minutes. Most within one.

"Who the—" Kee flashed from frustrated to furious.

"Mallinson," the Secretary stated. "He couldn't wait to get out of here."

"That's what you figured out," the President pointed at Linda.

"Right. His departure in the middle of the reception for a meeting was the piece that didn't fit. But I don't understand why he did it."

President Matthews laughed. It was bitter, but it was a laugh. "This one I know. The Secretary of State is fourth in line to the presidency. By the way, the first three were also in this room tonight. He was trying to stage a coup. A very bloody one."

"But the clues. Chinese, Japanese…"

"Whether they were a smokescreen or the attempt of a foreign power to gain power over our government, that will be someone else's problem to figure out. Tonight you protected the White House and this government. You are a credit to the force," the President's tone made it clear that was the end of that topic.

For a moment she wondered if he meant the Secret Service or the White House Protection Force—then understood that he meant both.

He held out his arm to her and she could only blink at him in surprise.

"We're late for dinner. And as my wife's flight from Vietnam is delayed, I believe that you are my date. I'll tell you about a rather nice ranch you and your boyfriend should visit in Montana someday."

With Thor's lead in one hand and former President Matthews' elbow in the other, she led the way down the Grand Staircase while she tried to digest the word "boyfriend."

EPILOGUE

"*I* found the words," she told Thor.

He licked her face, which made her glad about her staunch refusal to wear any makeup.

"You ready?" She scrubbed her fingers into his sides and he wiggled with delight. "Of course you are," she acknowledged in her squeaky dog voice.

"He's always ready," Dilya laughed. "He's a dog. How about you?"

Linda looked over at her. This time their dresses matched, or were at least color coordinated. Dilya had insisted and Linda had known better than to argue.

"You never were fifteen, were you?"

Dilya shrugged. She could pass for twenty-five in the elegant dress of pale-lavender silk with a wide white sash emphasizing her waist. She wore her hair down—the only styling battle that Linda had won in this entire affair other than no makeup. If Dilya's hair was down, then she could leave her own down as well.

"You're still short, you know," she teased Dilya.

"So are you!" Her maid of honor stuck her tongue out at Linda.

"Taller than you," Linda returned the salute with an added raspberry.

"Not much," Dilya pointed to her own bright red boots with two-inch heels.

Linda had won the shoe battle by arguing that she wanted to dance with her new husband and didn't want to trip. Dilya had finally caved and *allowed* her to purchase white flats, but it had cost her two inches in the height battle and left her with only a narrow lead.

There was a discreet knock. Dilya answered and then let former President Matthews into the room. Linda rose to her feet.

"You look very nice in your suit, President Matthews."

"That's Secretary of State Matthews, thanks to you. It's so good to have something useful to do. I can never show you my full appreciation for coming up with the idea. And you look amazing in that dress."

"Thank you. I had the best help ever," she placed a hand on Dilya's shoulder in thanks. Then she did a slow turn for him and he made a point of applauding. She watched herself in the East Bedroom mirror, a room that the First Family had loaned her for the occasion.

The wedding would be small, but the President and First Lady had insisted on holding it in the Residence's Central Hall where she'd saved everyone's lives three months before.

Dilya had understood her well enough to choose a simple white knee-length dress, with a lace sheer and a lavender waistband to match Dilya's dress.

She'd considered a bouquet of chocolate, then thought of apple blossoms instead. How perfect a gift Clive had given her.

"You know, I tried to perform the ceremony for Emily once."

"How did that turn out?"

Secretary Matthews grimaced. "Not well. I lost a shoe in her pond."

"No ponds here, you should be safe."

"I hope so. I like these shoes. Are you ready for this? If so, we should do it before the groom melts down like one of his chocolates."

She used a bit of lace to tie the rings onto Thor's harness.

Linda bit her lower lip for a moment, then nodded. As ready as she was ever going to be to completely change her life in a single moment.

Former President Matthews had been an obvious replacement for the jailed Secretary of State Mallinson. He knew global politics from his own two terms of office; because of his wife's directorship with the UNESCO World Heritage Centre, he had continued to travel widely, and he was immensely respected around the world—by both friend and foe. The way he had lit up the moment she'd suggested the idea over Clive's luscious dessert soup, she knew it had been one of her better ones.

"Oh, wait," Linda dug into her purse—because Dilya had finally won that war—and pulled out the thin gold ribbon. It was from the one chocolate bouquet she'd gotten to eat on that night a lifetime ago. She looked at the words on it for a moment.

Freedom and Unity.

It might be the Vermont motto, but it was also a good message for herself: freedom from her past and a new unity in her future. Tied up in a gold knot.

"Could you give this to him?"

Secretary Matthews took it cautiously, then read the words and smiled. Without comment, he stepped over and gave her a hug and a kiss on the forehead. He did the same for Dilya before heading out the door to get in place so that he could officiate the wedding ceremony of Linda and Clive Andrews. It would be a relief to be rid of her family name.

Dilya followed through the door when the pianist started the Wedding March on the grand piano. The First and Second families would be rising to their feet, along with Dilya's parents. Linda had decided against inviting her own—a choice Clive had agreed to after a brief, very brief, visit to Vermont. But there absolutely was a contingent from the Secret Service K-9 teams with their dogs.

She'd found a team as fine as the 75th Rangers. They gave her a place and a purpose.

Linda might not have recognized the vivacious older woman who had offered her services as photographer if not for her gold locket and piercing blue eyes. She was tall, with long silver hair, and looked slimly elegant in a black von Furstenberg pantsuit as she wielded her cameras. If Clive had caught on that it was Miss Watson, he certainly hadn't mentioned it.

Clive.

He was the one who had given her the greatest gift of all.

His patience and love.

It had taken her two months to find the words "I love you" inside herself. The moment she'd found them and managed to speak them (which had been a whole separate challenge), they'd both wept.

Then and there—while the tears still streamed down her face for only the second time since her childhood had ended—he had gone down on bent knee to propose.

Clive had given her a promise she'd never imagined possible.

He'd promised a future and a family.

She only had to find two more words to make it all come true. She'd already written "I do" on a piece of paper clutched in her fist just in case she couldn't say them aloud.

But she knew she would, and stepped out the door in confidence. She would walk down the aisle herself with Thor to escort her.

She'd be able to say them because, just like his chocolate, Clive's promises would turn out to be ever so perfectly delightful.

BONUS SCENE -EXCLUSIVELY FOR
NEWSLETTER SUBSCRIBERS

(ALREADY SUBSCRIBED? CHECK YOUR
LATEST NEWSLETTER FOR LINK.)

This scene occurs during the story *Off The Leash*,
but from Dilya's point of view.

*Dilya knew the future wasn't to be trusted. But could she even trust
her past?*

also receive:
Release News
Free Short Stories
a Free Book

Do it today. Do it now.
www.mlbuchman.com/dilya

ON YOUR MARK (EXCERPT)

IF YOU LIKED THIS, YOU'LL LOVE JIM AND
REESE. COMING FEB. 28, 2018. PRE-ORDER
IT NOW!

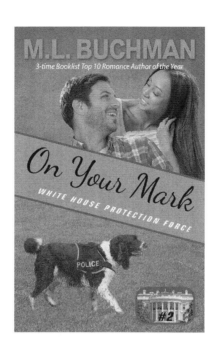

ON YOUR MARK (EXCERPT)

*M*alcolm was happier than a horned toad at a mayfly festival.

And when his English springer spaniel was happy, Jim was happy.

It was one of those impossibly clear days that Washington, DC dished out like dog treats in February. The hard winter nights were probably behind them. In another month, even the occasional below freezing nights would be nothing but a memory. Now it was an hour past sunrise, the temperature was already above forty, and the maples and beeches along the White House fence line looked as if the tips of their branches had been dusted with just the tiniest bit of bright green. The ornamental cherry trees were already dusted pink.

The air smelled fresh and vibrant with possibility. He loved the way that every city had its own smell and he'd now been in DC long enough, each season wrapped about him like fireflies on a summer evening with its own special particulars. He'd lived most of his life on the road in one way or another, but two years here just might be enough to anchor him in place for a lifetime.

He often wondered what Malcolm smelled on such days. The

189

freshening grass? The latest civilian dog pee-o-gram on a tree trunk? The track of the other US Secret Service PSCO explosives-sniffing dog currently on patrol?

Handling a USSS Personnel Screening Canine—Open Area, also known as a Friendly or Floppy-eared dog, around the White House perimeter was the best duty there ever was. He and Malcolm had been walking this beat for two years now, putting even the mailmen to shame. Just because a blizzard *and* a hurricane had ripped through last year, each shutting down the city, didn't mean the security at the White House put its feet up— at least not these six paws. The only things that had been moving in the whole area during either event were emergency services, the guards at the Tomb of the Unknown Soldier out at Arlington Cemetery, and White House security.

The snowstorm had been a doozy by DC standards, almost as deep as Malcolm's legs were long. The next morning had been a surprisingly busy day at the fence line as tourists had trudged through a foot of heavy, wet snow to get photos of the White House under a thick, white blanket. Most of the crazies had stayed warm in their beds that day.

Not even the worst of the crazies came out during the hurricane.

Today it was the sunshine *and* the madness that drew people to his patrol zone along the White House fence. Separating the two before Malcolm did had become one of his favorite games to occupy the time. He figured the visitors to the fence fell into five distinct categories, only two of which Malcolm was trained to give a hoot about.

The True Tourist. They would just stand and stare though the steel fence. It had been formed to look like the old wrought iron one, but was far stronger. These people were often the older set— marked at a distance by taking pictures of the White House rather than taking selfies of them *at* the White House.

The Clickbait Tourist. They'd barely glance at the magnificent building. But even if they never actually looked at it, everyone inundated by their social media feeds more than made up for the lack.

The Squared-away Vet. The ex-military who arrived to see the representation of everything they had given. Whether standing tall or rolling along in a wheelchair, they came to see, to understand. He liked talking to them when he could. Jim had done his dance. Nothing fancy—a "heavy" driver for three tours hauling everything from pallets of Coca-Cola to Abrams tanks.

The Mad Vets and the Crazies. These guys were damaged. The less toxic ones just wanted to tell their story to the President so that he "really" understood. But there was a sliding scale right up to the ones who wanted retribution. These were the fence jumpers. They might have a protest sign, an aluminum foil hat, a .45 tucked in their pocket, or a load of righteous wrath strapped to their bodies. No real plot or plan, they were solo actors and had to be picked off one at a time. He and Malcolm caught their fair share of those—maybe more because Malcolm was such an awesome explosives detection dog. These were the main target of the fence patrol.

The Terrorist. Bottom line, that's why his team and all of the others were here even with them all knowing they were, at best, an early warning of any concerted attack. They'd all seen the movies *White House Down* and *Olympus Has Fallen*. It was amazing how much Hollywood could get wrong and still scare the crap out of you—definitely not entertainment to anyone who worked guarding the White House. They discussed worst-case scenarios all the time. And he sure prayed that it didn't happen until after he was dead and buried—though he'd wager that he could be pissed just fine from the grave.

It was still early enough in the day that the fence line was almost exclusively the top three categories. The Mad Vet and the Crazies category typically didn't kick in hard until later in the day when their morning meds wore off.

He saw a Squared-away Vet standing at the fence. The officers were particularly easy to pick out. They liked everything in order and would instinctively find the exact centerline—at either Lafayette Square to the north or the curving line of the President's Park to the south. As predictable as sunshine on a clear day, they would come to a halt at precisely the twelve or six o'clock positions and simply stare.

Normally they didn't notice him or react if they did. This one stared at him...no, at Malcolm with eyes so wide it was a wonder that they remained in his head.

"*Gute hund*," he instructed Malcolm—training him in German avoided confusion with an alert word accidentally spoken in a sentence. He'd met a dog once trained with the numbers in Japanese: *Ichi*—sit. *Ni*—stay. *San*—down. *Shi*—heel... Pretty darn slick. He'd thought about retraining Malcolm to be bilingual for the fun of it, but it seemed a dirty trick to play on a perfectly nice dog.

Gute hund—good dog—told Malcolm he was off duty and could relax and be a dog for a moment rather than a sniffing magician.

It also gave Jim an excuse to let Malcolm approach and really check out the veteran up close just in case he was a Crazy-in-disguise. Even "off duty" Malcolm would respond if he smelled something dangerous.

Nope, guy was clean.

Jim glanced back at his patrol partner and nodded to indicate he'd be stopping for a moment. PSCO dogs never worked the fence line alone. Sergeant Mickey Claremont followed five to ten meters behind him. He was a big guy, looking even more so because of the bulletproof vest over his warm coat clearly labeled USSS Police. The AR-15 automatic rifle that he carried across his chest was part of his primary duty of being backup in case Malcolm did alert to someone. His second job included making sure that nothing slowed Jim's and Malcolm's progress. But

Claremont had learned that there were certain types of guys that Jim always stopped for.

"You handled dogs?" He asked the wide-eyed vet hovering uncertainly at the fence.

All he managed was a nod back.

"Been out long?"

Head shake...then a grimace.

"Don't worry about it, brother. The words will come back eventually."

"You sure?" Barely a whisper and now the guy was watching him.

"Three tours in the Dustbowl. Nothing fancy. A heavy driver on the Kandahar and Kabul run." A fellow soldier would know what that meant. Hauling heavy loads, desperately needed by the in-country teams, from the port at Karachi, Pakistan, across a thousand kilometers to Kandahar, Afghanistan, or another five hundred clicks to Kabul. And every millimeter past the southern Wesh-Chaman border' crossing or the Torkham one to the north had been run in constant fear of being a giant target on a known road. They'd lost a lot of guys, but he'd made it out in one piece.

"Two tours in Baghdad. One in Mosul," the guy at the fence was back to staring at Malcolm. He reached out a tentative hand as if he was seeing a ghost, but pulled it back before he could test the theory.

"That's some hard shit, brother," Jim wouldn't have wanted that tour any day. "Just give yourself some time."

The guy nodded, almost desperately.

"Hit the support groups," Jim dug out a card from the stack he always carried and handed it over. "These guys saved my ass. Gotta get back to work now. Good luck, buddy. *Such!*" Like *soock* with a guttural German *ck—Seek!* And Malcolm went back to sniffing his way along the fence line. Even letting the guy know that there was such a thing as "getting back to work" would help.

Claremont folded in behind him and worked the second part of his job as they passed more tourists.

"Yes, he's a bomb-sniffing dog." "No, you can't pet him because he's working right now." "Yes, it's okay to take his picture but, no, he can't pose for a picture because he's working right now." And so on in an unending litany.

Jim was so used to it that the silence always seemed wrong after the crowds thinned out at night but the patrols continued.

They were nearing their one-hour limit. A dog's nose only went so long without a break. One hour on, half-hour off. Which was good, that gave him enough time to do the paperwork that was part of being a PSCO handler: patrol reports, daily security briefing, studying the faces of known risk agents and recent threats. A letter writer was usually just that, someone dumb enough to threaten the President's life and then put their return address on the envelope. A single visit from the Secret Service was usually enough to scare those dummies back under the wire. But it didn't hurt to have studied their faces in case they transitioned to The Crazies category.

That's when he spotted the sixth type of visitor to the White House fence—The Newbie.

REESE CARVER STOOD at the White House fence and tried to figure out what had changed.

Actually, she knew exactly what had changed, but she couldn't reconcile how different it *felt*. Four years driving for the Secret Service, that last year in the Presidential Motorcade, and still she wasn't ready for the scale of this morning's change.

It was the same White House she'd pulled up to a hundred times before.

At first she'd waited outside the gate in one of the escort vehicles.

Then they'd started bouncing her around: press corps van, support vehicles for carrying the staff who didn't rate a ride in the President's car or one of the spares, then command and control while the guys in the back handled route logistics on the fly, and even the front sweep car that checked the route out ahead of the motorcade.

Hazmat had been hard on her nerves because she knew nothing about what those guys actually did.

Watchtower—the electronic countermeasures vehicle capable of suppressing remote explosive triggers, and laser and radar detection of incoming threats—had made her feel like she was constantly being irradiated. It was also a mobile cell tower, satellite uplink, and everything else imaginable.

She'd even driven Halfback—the lethal Chevy Suburban that carried the protection detail immediately behind the President's limo. She'd liked that one. The agents were armed to the gills, including a pop-up-through-the-roof Minigun. Could have used that back on the NASCAR race tracks a few times on some of the assholes who thought ganging up to shut out a female driver was good sport.

With all these different assignments, it had gotten to the point where she'd driven every vehicle except for Stagecoach—the Presidential monster itself, also nicknamed The Beast for a reason —and the ambulance that always trailed along behind.

She'd liked driving the unimaginatively named Spares. The two identical copies of the Presidential limousine played a constant shuttle game with Stagecoach so that a terrorist would never be sure which vehicle carried the President and which was the decoy. Any Spare driver worth their salt dreamed of Stagecoach breaking down and the President shifting into their vehicle—which had happened only five times in the last two decades, so the chances were low.

Then she'd crossed the Motorcade drivers' "finish line."

The Secret Service had hundreds of elite drivers, from the San

Francisco SWAT team to the Capital Police of the Uniformed Division. The competition to reach the Presidential Motorcade had been fierce.

Just this morning she'd gotten a wake-up call from the head of the Presidential Protection Detail, Senior Special Agent Harvey Lieber.

"Bumping you to driving Stagecoach, Reese. Get your ass in here." With Lieber, that wasn't some slur because she was a black woman with an ass that she'd been complimented on far too many times. All it meant was for her to get her ass in there. From him, she'd take that, but not from any other asshole.

That call had changed the world.

A part of her was ready to do a victory dance.

Reese Carver—the first woman to drive The Beast. And a black woman at that. She wanted to do her dance on the heads of every male idiot that said a woman couldn't do it. Every jerk who'd tried to put her down—even after she'd smeared them off the track. She'd learned the hard way to keep it all inside. Men were expected to brag, but one little smile out of place and it tagged a woman as a bitch. Fine. Whatever.

But the other part of her could only stand and stare at the White House. Next time she drove onto the grounds, it wouldn't be a matter of escorting the President. Next time his life would be in her hands.

"What am I supposed to feel about that?" She didn't have a clue.

"First days are always like that," a deep baritone said from close beside her.

"What?" She turned and looked up at the blue-eyed UD smiling at her. The Secret Service Uniformed Division guys always struck her as a little foolish. Didn't they get it? United States Secret Service meant Special Agent. Secrecy. Not parading around Washington, DC dressed like a cop. They really should be called something else. Maybe—as they *were* standing on the edge of the National Mall—they should rename them Mall cops. She liked that. She'd didn't come up with funny things on her own very often, but that wasn't half bad.

"Your first day?" He nodded toward the White House in a friendly fashion. His smile said that he was completely assured of his own charm. She'd never yet met a man like that who actually charmed her.

"Not even close," she warned him off.

"Oh," his smile didn't diminish. "You have the look."

"What look?" She didn't have a look. No one was supposed to be able to see what she was feeling. She'd learned that lesson the hard way a long time ago. "Like some lost fem in search of a big, strong, handsome man to protect her?"

He laughed. "Like you can see the White House, but it's spooking the crap out of you worse than a mouse at a cat convention. See that a lot on Newbies."

"Not." Keep it short. Make him go away. Nobody saw through her shields like that—so not allowed. She looked away and down into the big brown eyes of a smiling springer spaniel. He was standing there looking up at her with his tongue lolling out. She reached out to pet him.

And he sat abruptly.

Reese froze.

It was the signal that explosive-detection dogs used to alert their handler that they'd found something. Out of the corner of her eye she saw the backup man shift his grip on his AR-15 semi-auto as he moved for a better angle. Tourists continued streaming by as if nothing was amiss.

She straightened very slowly, keeping her hands in clear view.

Keep reading. Available at fine retailers everywhere.
Find it now!

ABOUT THE AUTHOR

M.L. Buchman started the first of, what is now over 50 novels and as many short stories, while flying from South Korea to ride his bicycle across the Australian Outback. Part of a solo around the world trip that ultimately launched his writing career.

All three of his military romantic suspense series—The Night Stalkers, Firehawks, and Delta Force—have had a title named "Top 10 Romance of the Year" by the American Library Association's *Booklist*. NPR and Barnes & Noble have named other titles "Top 5 Romance of the Year." In 2016 he was a finalist for Romance Writers of America prestigious RITA award. He also writes: contemporary romance, thrillers, and fantasy.

Past lives include: years as a project manager, rebuilding and single-handing a fifty-foot sailboat, both flying and jumping out of airplanes, and he has designed and built two houses. He is now making his living as a full-time writer on the Oregon Coast with his beloved wife and is constantly amazed at what you can do with a degree in Geophysics. You may keep up with his writing and receive a free starter e-library by subscribing to his newsletter at: www.mlbuchman.com

Join the conversation:
www.mlbuchman.com

Other works by M. L. Buchman:

The Night Stalkers

MAIN FLIGHT
The Night Is Mine
I Own the Dawn
Wait Until Dark
Take Over at Midnight
Light Up the Night
Bring On the Dusk
By Break of Day

WHITE HOUSE HOLIDAY
Daniel's Christmas
Frank's Independence Day
Peter's Christmas
Zachary's Christmas
Roy's Independence Day
Damien's Christmas

AND THE NAVY
Christmas at Steel Beach
Christmas at Peleliu Cove

5E
Target of the Heart
Target Lock on Love
Target of Mine

Firehawks

MAIN FLIGHT
Pure Heat
Full Blaze
Hot Point
Flash of Fire
Wild Fire

SMOKEJUMPERS
Wildfire at Dawn
Wildfire at Larch Creek
Wildfire on the Skagit

Delta Force
Target Engaged
Heart Strike
Wild Justice

Where Dreams
Where Dreams are Born
Where Dreams Reside
Where Dreams Are of Christmas
Where Dreams Unfold
Where Dreams Are Written

Eagle Cove
Return to Eagle Cove
Recipe for Eagle Cove
Longing for Eagle Cove
Keepsake for Eagle Cove

Henderson's Ranch
Nathan's Big Sky
Big Sky, Loyal Heart

Love Abroad
Heart of the Cotswolds: England

Dead Chef Thrillers
Swap Out!
One Chef!
Two Chef!

Deities Anonymous
Cookbook from Hell: Reheated
Saviors 101

SF/F Titles
The Nara Reaction
Monk's Maze
the Me and Elsie Chronicles

Strategies for Success (NF)
Managing Your Inner Artist/Writer
Estate Planning for Authors

SIGN UP FOR M. L. BUCHMAN'S NEWSLETTER TODAY

and receive:
Release News
Free Short Stories
a Free Book

Get your free book today. Do it now.
free-book.mlbuchman.com

Printed in Great Britain
by Amazon